"Move your big paw and let me out of here!"
Eden demanded, her green eyes flashing.

"No," Mark said, inching closer to her, trapping her securely in place, but not touching her body with any part of his.

"I'm warning you—" she said, damning the trembling in her voice and in her knees.

"What's wrong, Eden? Is it that you wanted more than a kiss? You wanted me? Because I wanted you. I still want you. My body is aching for you. I don't usually lose control, lady, but you took me to the brink. You pushed some invisible button inside me that I didn't know existed." He kissed one side of her mouth, then the other. "Did you feel it? The heat, the desire burning in me, in you, us, together?"

"No," she whispered. But her body was still thrumming with heated desire, and she knew she'd never forget the taste, the scent, the feel of Mark, as long as she lived.

WHAT ARE *LOVESWEPT* ROMANCES?

They are stories of true romance and touching emotion. We believe those two very important ingredients are constants in our highly sensual and very believable stories in the *LOVESWEPT* line. Our goal is to give you, the reader, stories of consistently high quality that may sometimes make you laugh, sometimes make you cry, but are always fresh and creative and contain many delightful surprises within their pages.

Most romance fans read an enormous number of books. Those they truly love, they keep. Others may be traded with friends and soon forgotten. We hope that each *LOVESWEPT* romance will be a treasure—a "keeper." We will always try to publish

LOVE STORIES YOU'LL NEVER FORGET
BY AUTHORS YOU'LL ALWAYS REMEMBER

The Editors

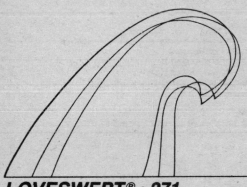

LOVESWEPT® · 271
Joan Elliott Pickart
Tattered Wings

BANTAM BOOKS
TORONTO · NEW YORK · LONDON · SYDNEY · AUCKLAND

TATTERED WINGS

A Bantam Book / August 1988

If you would be interested in receiving protective vinyl
covers for your Loveswept books, please write to this address
for information:

Loveswept
Bantam Books
P.O. Box 985
Hicksville, NY 11802

ISBN 0-553-21912-X

Published simultaneously in the United States and Canada

Bantam Books are published by Bantam Books, a division
of Bantam Doubleday Dell Publishing Group, Inc. Its trademark, consisting of the words "Bantam Books" and the
portrayal of a rooster, is Registered in U.S. Patent and
Trademark Office and in other countries. Marca Registrada.
Bantam Books, 666 Fifth Avenue, New York, New York 10103.

PRINTED IN THE UNITED STATES OF AMERICA

O   0 9 8 7 6 5 4 3 2 1

In memory of Lesli Stryker

One

Mark Hampton parked his car in the space that had his last name painted in carefully stenciled black letters on the curb. He turned off the ignition, folded his arms on top of the steering wheel, and gazed at the tall trees beyond the parking lot. A chill wind tore a multitude of the dry, colored leaves from the branches, swirled them into a frenzy, then released them, allowing them to fall in a vibrant cascade of color.

Winter was on its way, Mark thought, getting out of the car. He started slowly across the concrete lot, glancing again at the falling leaves. And winter in Washington, D.C., was ugly. Oh, the first snowfall was beautiful, transforming the nation's capital into a white, shimmering fairyland. But after that? It was dirty slush, dreary skies, and biting cold. Ugly. His knee ached in the damp winter of D.C., too. Ached like hell.

Spring was nice. Spring brought the cherry blossoms and green grass. He liked spring, and he liked autumn, with the leaves that glowed such vivid reds and golds. Summer, however, was an ongoing humidity-induced sweat. So the Hampton vote was in. Spring and autumn were acceptable in Washington, D.C. Summer and winter stunk.

And he, Mark admitted to himself, was in a strange and crummy mood. Well, Monday was not his favorite day of the week. Oh, terrific, he thought. What was next? An in-depth study to see how he felt about Tuesday, Wednesday, the rest of the week? Enough was enough. He'd better shape up his mood pronto, or he would be in for a very long day.

As he approached the side entrance to the nondescript gray building, two uniformed men snapped to attention and saluted crisply. Mark returned the salutes with less enthusiasm and nodded his thanks as one of the men pulled the door open for him.

"Good morning, Colonel," the young man said.

" 'Morning," Mark said. "It's nippy this morning."

"Yes, sir. It certainly is, sir. Have a nice day."

"Right," Mark said. Kids, he thought, striding down the brightly lit corridor. They looked like kids who should be cruising the streets in shiny cars, whistling at pretty girls. If he'd told the boy at the door it was a beautiful day, warm enough to take a dip in the Potomac, the kid would have said, "Yes, sir. It certainly is, sir." What music it would be to hear "Are you crazy, sir? I'm freezing my buns off out here." Never happen.

Mark shook his head, smiling at his own foolishness, then turned a corner and walked down another hall. At the end, he opened a door and was greeted by the snap to attention and salute of his aide, Airman Norman Fifer.

"Good morning, Colonel."

"Norm," Mark said, not bothering to return the salute. "Any calls?"

"Yes, sir. General Meyers wants to see you in his office the minute you arrive."

"I love Mondays," Mark said dryly. He crossed the room and opened the door to his office. "It's such a challenge trying to survive them."

"Yes, sir," the airman said. "Shall I call and say you're on your way?"

Mark stepped into his office, placed his billed cap on top of the filing cabinet, and returned to the outer office.

"I'm on my way," he said.

"But should I call and tell the general's secretary you're on your way?"

"Good idea, Norm. You're sharp as a tack this morning."

"Thank you, sir," Norm said, smiling brightly. He snatched up the telephone receiver.

Mark rolled his eyes and left the office. Where did they get these gung-ho kids? he wondered. Well, he'd probably been a gung-ho kid himself many years ago. But not for long. There had been a war going on in a charming little place called Vietnam. Boys became men very quickly in those days. And boys became dead very quickly then too. Damn, he really was in a weird mood. The coming of winter and a Monday morning were a lethal combination.

As Mark headed toward the general's office, he reached in his pocket for the plastic-coated clip-on badge that would gain him entry to the other side of the building. He attached it to the flap of his pocket and automatically returned the salutes of two more very young airmen on duty at the end of the long corridor.

"Good morning, Colonel," one said.

"No, it isn't," Mark said pleasantly.

"Yes, sir," the airman said.

Mark chuckled softly and proceeded to the general's office.

General Meyers's secretary was a tall, beautiful lieutenant named Kathleen. The way she filled out her uniform often made Mark wonder if there was a regulation against it somewhere. She had a subtle, sensuous way of letting him know she was very interested in him, but he'd never pursued the sexy Kathleen during the three years he'd been stationed in D.C. She kept trying, and he kept ignoring, and on it went like a game. Ridiculous.

"Hello, Colonel," Kathleen said, scanning him from the shoelaces up before meeting his gaze. "It's cold outside this morning."

"Really?" he said, flashing her a dazzling smile. "I didn't notice."

"Winter is coming. It makes me think of cozy fires, soft music, snifters of expensive brandy."

"No kidding," Mark said. "I think of slush and slop and wonder whether my car will start. The general is expecting me."

Kathleen glared at him. "Go right in . . . sir."

"You're ever so kind. Keep up the good work, Lieutenant. Your country is proud of you."

"Bull," she said under her breath.

Mark laughed, knocked once on the general's door, and entered.

"Come in, Mark," General Meyers said, waving him forward, "but shut the door. You know Colonel Jim Kinney."

"Jim," Mark said. "How's life?"

"Lousy." Jim Kinney was forty-five, short, stocky, and rapidly losing his hair. He was also, on this Monday morning with winter approaching, looking none too happy.

Mark sensed trouble.

"We've got trouble," General Meyers said. "Pour yourself a cup of coffee, Mark, and get comfortable."

The two colonels settled into chairs opposite General Meyers's desk. Mark blew on the steaming liquid in his cup, then took a sip of the strong, bitter coffee. He propped one ankle on his other knee and waited.

"Mark," General Meyers said, after a long moment of silence, "You know, of course, about Project Unicorn, since you head the security clearance section."

Mark nodded. "I do, but I didn't clear any of the personnel working on it. It was in full operation before I transferred here. In fact, I've never seen the files on the Unicorn team. All I really know is that it's Jim's baby."

"I'm aware that it was set up before you came," General Meyers said, "but you've got security clearance to know what Project Unicorn is. Have you ever looked into what it entails?"

"No. I have enough on my plate without poking my nose into things that were squared away before I got here."

"Well, you're in it now, buddy," Jim said. "One of my key people is missing."

Mark dropped his propped foot to the floor and straightened in his chair. "Missing?"

"As in, no one can find him." Jim shook his head. "Lord, why me? Okay, in a nutshell, Mark. Project Unicorn is a top-secret, gold-star security clearance level project that's been in operation for five years under my command. I have a team of six computer programmers developing a system for picking up and unscrambling coded messages sent by satellite from one foreign country to another. It's really coming together now. We're just about there."

"I'm impressed," Mark said. "There are a lot of interesting conversations being transmitted in code by satellite, I imagine. First guys out of the chute would have a real edge."

"Exactly," Jim said. "My people have been pushing because the end is in sight. We're close, damn close, to testing this program. Everyone has been picking up satellite messages for a long time. We've discovered layered codes, highly sophisticated means of transmission, and now we'll have the program to decipher them. What this could mean to our country's security is mind-boggling."

"And?" Mark asked, leaning forward in his chair.

Jim shook his head again. "I should have seen it, I suppose. As I said, my team has been pushing, putting in long hours. Last week my team leader, Captain William Johnson, came to me and said he was burned out. He couldn't sleep, was having trouble concentrating, his appetite was gone. He said he had to have a few days off to clear his head before he blew a mental fuse."

"That happens," Mark said. "I assume you told him to go for it?"

"Of course. I just wish I'd paid closer attention, seen the stress signs before he was in that bad shape. Anyway, he left Friday night for a dude ranch, or whatever the hell it is, in Montana. Bill said it was exactly what he needed. He'd hike, ride horses, just get away from it all. He said he'd be back this morning."

"But no Bill Johnson," Mark said.

"Nope. I got a call from a Miss Landry at that dude ranch, the Lazy L it's called, at one this morning. She said Bill had set off yesterday afternoon on a horse and the horse came back at dark. No Bill. She called in the local sheriff and they started a search. At one A.M., when Bill had been gone twelve hours, she pulled his registration card. He has no family and had put me down as the person to notify in case of an emergency. I said I'd check back with her after the search party had gone further at dawn. Nothing. There's no trace of him."

"Did this Miss Landry indicate she knew from Bill's registration card that he was in the Air Force?" Mark asked.

"No. She seemed rather startled when I answered the phone with my rank. Apparently Bill didn't put that on the card either. She said something about Bill listing himself as a government employee in D.C., and she supposed it made sense that he knew military people. I didn't tell her he was an Air Force captain."

"Jim," Mark asked, "do you know if Bill is an experienced rider? Has he gone on leave to the wilds before?"

Jim nodded. "That's his thing. The guy is a computer genius and sort of an eccentric. When he's concentrating on a program, you might as well be talking to the wall. When he needs to unwind he goes off by himself to some remote place. That Miss Landry from the Lazy L was shook up. She said Bill had assured her he was an experienced rider, expert in wilderness survival, all of that. Otherwise, she never would have let him go off by himself." He paused. "And are you ready for this? They had a light snow there last night."

"Oh, great," Mark said. "There go any tracks Bill might have left. So? What do you want *me* to do?" He switched his gaze to General Meyers. "No, let me guess. You want me to go find him."

"Got it in one," the general said. "You were Air Force Intelligence as a pilot *and* on the ground, Mark. You have the training for this. Not only in actual tracking in rough country, but you know how to get information out of people. That's why you're head of security clearance here. You have that sixth sense we need for this. Your service record says so, and so do all those ribbons on your chest."

"Look," Mark said, "if Bill Johnson is as experienced as you say in wilderness survival, he's liable to walk into that dude ranch any minute asking for his breakfast. Can't we wait it out a bit?"

"Too risky," Jim said. "Johnson has the last part of the computer program for Project Unicorn."

"He has it? With him? You just let him stroll out the door with it?"

Jim tapped his temple with one finger. "He has it in his head, Mark. The guy is a genius, remember? I'd bet my pension he could duplicate the entire program, then add the final piece to the puzzle, which only he knows at this point."

"Hell," Mark said, slouching back in his chair.

Jim went on. "Bill told me he needed a couple of days off before he put the last section into the master computer system. He was afraid he'd make a mistake if he tried it without a break in routine first. I didn't question him. I've worked with these people a long time. This isn't the first time one of them wanted a breather. They go off for a couple of days, then show up as good as new."

Mark frowned and rubbed his hand over his chin. "Not this time."

"That's why we called you in, Mark," General Meyers said. "Maybe Johnson just dug in somewhere when it started to snow. But . . ."

"But maybe he didn't."

"Exactly. It's the timing of the thing that has me concerned. Johnson literally has Project Unicorn with him. I'd rather overreact than sit on our butts and hope he shows. I want you to go to Montana, Mark, and take over the search. Arrive in uniform and act as though it's standard procedure for the military to step in when one of their own is missing. I doubt anyone in a remote part of Montana is going to question it. There's no reason for them to suspect this is a highly volatile situation. You simply bark orders and scowl at the local sheriff's crew like you're used to ordering civilians around when the occasion arises."

"They don't know that Bill is Air Force."

"They will when you get there. You can wear whatever you like to go tracking through the mountains, but I want you to arrive like General Patton. Don't give anyone time to question your authority. And don't tell me we're not playing this by the book.

There are a few reprimand write-ups in your file from the times you chose to forget the book existed."

"I got the job done those times."

"And I want you to get it done this time," the general said. "Bring Bill Johnson back here. Your plane leaves in two hours. There will be a car reserved for you at the airport when you get to Montana. Jim, call that Miss Landry. Get directions to the ranch for Mark. Tell her a government specialist will be there by tonight. Don't say military, just government. Mark, what else?"

"Twenty-four-hour guards on the rest of the Project Unicorn team," Mark said. "That includes you, Jim. It's a safety precaution, not doubt about your integrity or anyone else's. I also want a report on Miss Landry, the Lazy L staff, and the local sheriff and his deputies out there. I'll call in tonight from the ranch to see what you have. I'll need copies of the security clearance files on the entire Unicorn team to read on the plane. Let's get a new secure phone line into your private office, too, General. The fewer people who know about this, the better. In fact, I think the Project Unicorn team should bunk here in the building until I have something to report."

"Done," the general replied, nodding. "I'll have the phone number for the new line before you leave."

"I can't believe this," Jim said. "It's like a nightmare."

"It may be a bunch of hoopla over nothing," Mark said, "but better safe than sorry. We've got a guy walking around out there with a top-secret military project in his head. The security setup on Unicorn stinks. I'm sorry, Jim, but it does. It should never have come to this."

"I wish you'd been around when Project Unicorn started," Jim said.

"Well, he wasn't," General Meyers said, "and neither was I. But it'll be my backside if there's something fishy going on here. All right, gentlemen, we have the wheels in motion. Jim, I'll send security people home with your team to have them pack, then come back here. No one will question that. We'll get the phone line in, and there will be strict orders that no one is to answer that phone if I'm not here. I'll expect to hear from you tonight, Mark."

Mark stood up. "You will. I've got to secure my office, then I'll come back here for the new phone number and to pick up the Unicorn personnel files. Jim, relax. Stewing isn't going to help. Hell, Johnson will probably be sitting by the fire when I get there."

"Then haul his butt back here," Jim said.

"Guaranteed. I knew this was going to be a crummy Monday."

"At least," General Meyers said, "you don't have to make the telephone call I'm about to."

"What call?" Mark asked.

"To the President."

"Oh, boy," Mark said, heading for the door. "I'm out of here."

General Meyers laughed. "I'll tell him not to worry about a thing because Colonel Mark Hampton has been put in charge of the situation."

"Wonderful," Mark said. "Some Mondays it just doesn't pay to get out of bed."

"That's the truth," Jim said glumly, following Mark from the office.

Mark stopped at Kathleen's desk as Jim continued on his way.

"We've got to stop meeting like this, Kathleen," he said. "There are rumors, you know."

"Cute," she said, not looking at him.

"Tsk tsk, have you no respect? Lieutenants are supposed to be awesomely in awe of colonels. It's in the handbook."

"Really?" She looked up at him and batted her eyelashes in an exaggerated fashion. "Well, Colonel, don't you think it's your patriotic duty to give me a refresher course on the handbook? Say, over dinner?"

"No can do," he said, striding toward the door. "Tonight is my class."

"What class?"

"On how to quit smoking."

"You don't smoke," she called after him.

"See?" he hollered from the hall. "It's a great class."

"Bull . . . sir!"

Mark laughed, then quickened his step as he glanced at his watch. Now that he really thought about it, he rather enjoyed the constant nonsense with Kathleen. They kept it in its proper place, never stepping over the line of military regulations or engaging in verbal sparring in front of the wrong people. Yes, lovely Kathleen was A-okay.

And thinking about her was a helluva lot better than mentally squaring off against this mess he was suddenly in. Where in the blue blazes was Captain William Johnson?

Mark entered his outer office and motioned to Norm to follow him. He sat down behind his desk while Norm stood at attention in front of it.

Mark glanced up. "Relax, Airman."

"Yes, sir."

"I've got to leave town for a while," Mark said, fanning out a half-dozen files on his desk.

"Yes, sir."

Mark leaned back in his chair and laced his fingers behind his head. "When you take my calls, simply get messages. If anyone hassles you, refer them to General Meyers."

"Yes, sir."

"These files on my desk can go over to Major Clemens."

"Yes, sir." He scooped up the files, then stood at attention again.

Mark sighed. "Norm, you're going to wear out your bones standing that stiffly all the time. It really isn't necessary."

"But, sir, the handbook—"

"Never mind," Mark said. "I'll be locking my office. General Meyers has the other key. I really don't know how long I'll be gone, Norm. Try not to die of boredom while I'm away."

"Yes, sir. I mean, no sir."

"Fine. Take those files over to Major Clemens."

"Now?"

"Yes, Norm. Now."

"Yes, sir," the airman said, and spun on his heel and left the room.

Mark shook his head. "That kid is exhausting." He picked up two more files and crossed the room to the filing cabinet. After locking the files inside, he put on his cap, then hesitated.

His gaze fell on a sleek metal model of a F-14 fighter jet on top of the filling cabinet. He drew a fingertip over the body of the plane and out along one wing, memories flooding over him.

He still missed it, he thought. Lord, how he loved to fly. He went up occasionally in a rented Cessna or Piper Cub, but there was nothing like the feel of an Air Force jet coming alive under his hands, taking him to the heavens, soaring higher, faster, responding to his touch like a willing woman. Once a fly-boy, always a fly-boy. It was in his blood forever. When this screwup with Johnson was straightened out, he'd rent a Piper and go for an entire day. But it wouldn't be the same as a jet. It wouldn't be like it once had been.

He tapped the model with his finger. "Keep your wings on, honey," he said, then turned and left the office, shutting off the light and locking the door behind him.

Mark glanced again at the directions to the Lazy L. It was late afternoon, and the sky was heavy with dark clouds that appeared all too ready to dump a load of snow. He'd driven twenty-five miles from the last town along a deserted paved road, another ten on a dirt stretch, and should soon be coming up on the Lazy L Ranch.

He went around a curve and saw an archway of twisted iron with "Lazy L" worked into it spanning the road. As he drove through the gates, he noticed a large, one-story ranch-style house in the distance, a red barn, pristine white corral fences, and about ten small cabins scattered around. There was also another slightly bigger cabin and a cluster of what appeared to be small storage sheds.

The Lazy L Ranch was a big operation, he realized. It would take a lot of money to keep up a place like this. Bill Johnson went first-class when he opted for time to clear his head.

Mark pulled up in front of the house, turned off the ignition, and got out of the car. The air had gone beyond crisp to definitely ice-cold, and he wasted no time covering the distance to the house. He sprinted up the four steps, crossed the porch, and knocked on the door.

"General Patton at your service, ma'am," he muttered. He straightened, cleared his throat, and plastered his best "I am a colonel, you dolt" expression on his face. He knocked again with more force.

The door was opened, and he found himself breathless. He was looking at one of the most beautiful women he'd ever seen. She was tall, maybe five-eight compared to his own six-feet-one. She had dark auburn hair that fell in waves to her shoulders, and her brilliant green eyes were like emeralds. Her skin looked like rich cream poured over perfectly molded features; her lips seemed to be begging to be kissed. She was dressed in faded jeans and a red-and-blue checked flannel shirt, both of which hugged her voluptuous body. Lord, she was gorgeous. And from the expression on her face, she wasn't thrilled out of her socks to see him.

"Miss Landry?"

"Yes."

"I'm Colonel Mark Hampton, United States Air Force." Dumb, Hampton, he thought. What did she think? He was with the Russian air force?

Well, big deal, Eden Landry thought. He certainly was impressed with his title, and probably his spiffy uniform too. Not that he didn't do it justice. Those were wonderfully broad shoulders on that tall frame, and blue did fabulous things for his gray eyes. She could see dark hair inching below his cap, and a smattering of gray above his ears. His face wasn't pretty-boy perfect, but rugged, craggy. The kind of face women looked twice at and the military put on recruiting posters. Oh, yes, he was handsome, this Colonel Mark Hampton, this blue-suiter standing on her porch, but she had more than enough on her mind without dealing with whatever it was he wanted.

"Miss Landry?" Mark repeated.

"What? Oh, yes, I'm sorry. What can I do for you, Colonel?"

Say now, Mark thought, that was an interesting question that conjured up all kinds of very interesting answers. He smiled at her. "You could invite me in out of the cold for starters."

Nice smile, Eden mused. Better than nice. It was a knock-em-dead smile. "Why?"

This was not going well, Mark thought. "Miss Landry," he said, striving for patience, "I'm here concerning the disappearance of Captain William Johnson. *Now* may I come in?"

"*Captain* Johnson?" She blinked. "Yes, of course, come in."

"Thank you," he said, welcoming the warmth of the room the moment he stepped inside. He removed his cap and tucked it under his arm as he glanced around the large living room. It was decorated in heavy dark furniture and vibrant colors, and a fire crackled in a huge stone fireplace on the far wall. He looked at Miss Landry again. "Yes, Captain Johnson, of the United States Air Force."

"I see. I didn't realize Mr. Johnson was in the military. His registration card didn't indicate that, and he never mentioned it. He listed his employer as the government."

"Which is true," Mark said, shrugging. "Do me a favor and tell me that Captain Johnson has come back and is no worse for wear."

Eden frowned. "No, there's been no sign of him. I went out on the first search, but I didn't go today because I had so much to do here. The snow has covered any tracks he might have left, and it looks like it's going to snow again. The sheriff is out there now with a search team. Please, come sit down. May I get you something? A drink? Warm or cold, whichever suits."

"Coffee, if you have it," he said. "Black. Has Captain Johnson ever stayed at the Lazy L before this weekend?"

"No, he hasn't. Make yourself comfortable. I'll be right back."

Mark watched her cross the room, his gaze missing no detail of her figure or the graceful way she moved. There was a subtle elegance about Miss Landry that spoke of high society and money, despite her rustic clothes. She really was beautiful.

And . . . And now that he thought about it, he had the feeling he'd seen her somewhere before.

In the kitchen Eden frowned when she saw that her hand was trembling as she poured coffee into two mugs.

It was the uniform, she told herself. The last thing she'd expected was to open her front door and find herself staring at a man in military uniform. Lord, the memories, the hateful, hurting memories, the sight of that uniform brought slamming into her mind. She couldn't handle this, not now, not when there was a man lost out there. She had no energy left, either physically or emotionally,* to deal with Colonel Mark Hampton of the United States Air Force. Lord, he sure got a charge out of saying all that. Did she look stupid, as though she'd think he was with the Russian Air Force or something? Well, one thing was for certain. He was going to drink his coffee, then haul his uniformed self out of there.

She returned to the living room and found him standing by the fire. She was struck again by his incredible good looks, ignored the flutter in the pit of her stomach, and crossed the room to hand him one of the mugs.

"Thank you," he said.

She settled onto a loveseat by the fire and watched as he lowered himself into a leather chair with smooth, athletic grace.

"Colonel . . ." she began.

"Mark."

"Mark, I want to assure you that everything is being done to locate Captain Johnson. Sheriff John Chambers and his deputies are highly trained in search and rescue operations. This is rough country. Hunters, hikers, and campers frequently get lost. So, if you'll tell me where you're staying in town, I'll notify you the moment Johnson is found."

Mark took a sip of the hot coffee, then peered at her for a long moment over the rim of the mug. Beautiful woman, he thought again. How he'd love to sink his hands into that gorgeous hair, lower his lips to hers, and . . .

He cleared his throat and shifted slightly as heat coursed through his lower body. Think like Patton, he told himself. Shape up, Hampton.

"I appreciate your reassurance, Miss Landry," he said. She really did look familiar. That was nuts. He'd never been to Montana before in his life. "However, I've come here to take charge of the search operation."

"I beg your pardon?"

"Captain Johnson is a member of the Air Force, Miss Landry. The Air Force is going to find him. It's very simple, really. I'll inform Sheriff Chambers of the change in command when he returns. If Captain Johnson is with him, that will take care of that. If not, I'll take over from here. When do you expect the search party to come in?"

Eden plunked her mug down on the end table and jumped to her feet. "Now, you wait just a darn minute here, Colonel," she said, planting her hands on her hips.

"Mark."

"Where are you stationed . . . Colonel?" she asked tightly.

Where had that question come from? he wondered. "Washington, D.C."

"Washington, D.C.," she repeated. "And I'm supposed to believe they sent a colonel all the way from D.C. because a captain is temporarily lost in the woods? And that this is standard operating procedure? You have no jurisdiction here, and you know it. You could join in the search for Captain Johnson, but you have no authority to take charge. This is private land, and Johnson was here on a short vacation, not a military mission. If John Chambers needs help, he'll call in the Montana National Guard. I don't know what's going on with your uninvited arrival, but don't try to snow me with your 'It's very simple really' line. You're out of order, mister, and I suggest you leave."

So much for General Patton, Mark thought. Damn, but Miss Landry was something when she got going. All spit and fire, her green eyes flashing like lasers. She had so much passion within her. Now it was channeled into anger, but he could imagine it turned to desire.

"What do you do?" he asked gruffly. "Read military handbooks instead of watching television?"

"I'm twenty-nine years old, Colonel. That's nearly twenty-nine years of first-hand knowledge of the Army. Oh, that's the Army of the United States of America, just in case you're wondering. I know the military . . . unfortunately. Not one thing you've said so far has added up."

"Well, I'm thirty-nine years old, Miss Landry," he said, setting his mug down beside hers. "It just could be that I know a little more than you do about military procedure. I'm taking charge here."

"The hell you are."

Slowly, Mark stood up. "What is your problem? I would think your first concern would be finding Captain Johnson. It can't help the reputation of this place to have your guests get lost. Why should you care who finds him, as long as the job is done?"

"Because I don't like your pushy military methods," she said, her voice rising. "And because I know you have no right to take over."

"Who was in the Army?" he asked quietly. "Your father?"

She crossed her arms protectively over her chest and took a step backward. "Yes," she said. "And my brother."

"Where are they?"

"Dead. They're both dead. I buried both of them in their uniforms. I have two folded flags, one for each. Those flags are supposed to comfort me, you see. Well, guess what? They don't. I'm loyal to my country, Colonel, but I don't care for the military philosophy. And I don't want to have a blue-suiter standing in my living room. I'd like you to leave."

"I'm sorry about your father and brother, Miss Landry, and I'm also sorry that my presence here disturbs and upsets you. But I can't leave." He ran his hand over the back of his neck. "It's imperative that Johnson be found as quickly as possible."

"There's a lot you're not telling me."

"I realize that. I'd hoped to come in here and take over without anyone questioning it. I didn't count on running into an Army brat who cut her teeth on the military handbook. Do you think we could sit down and discuss this calmly? And maybe"—he smiled at her—"we could be on a first-name basis. Except I don't even know your first name."

She sighed. "Eden."

"Eden," he repeated thoughtfully. He sat again in the leather chair as Eden took her place on the loveseat. "Eden," he said again, rubbing his hand over his chin. "Of course. That's why you look familiar. Your face is on magazine covers. There's Eden sportswear and evening wear, Eden perfume, and Lord only knows what else."

"That was a long time ago, Colonel . . . Mark. I run the Lazy L now."

"Eden products are still in the stores."

"True, but the display photographs of me are five years old."

"You haven't changed."

"Yes," she said quietly, "I have. Oh, maybe not physically, but I've changed. I left that world and I'm never going back."

"Why?"

"It's a long story. I see you have wings among your many other decorations. I assume you're a pilot for the Air Force?"

"No, not anymore."

"Why?"

He absently rubbed his right knee. "It's a long story."

"So cautious, aren't we?" she said, her voice still soft. "People are like that everywhere. They reveal just so much of themselves, then pull back, waiting, watching to see if this is someone they can trust. It's rather sad, but necessary."

"I guess I never thought about it," Mark said, looking at her intently. She suddenly seemed fragile, small, in need of protection. He wanted to pull her into his arms and chase the shadows of unhappiness from her lovely eyes. Why was she in the middle of nowhere in Montana? She must have had the world at her fingertips, yet she'd walked away from it all. Why? Strangely, he wanted to know everything about this exquisite creature. He had no idea why, but it was important to him that Eden smile again.

She was tired, that was all, Eden told herself.

That was the reason she had the urge to nestle into Mark Hampton's embrace, to feel his strong arms enfold her in a safe, comforting cocoon of strength and warmth. There was a vitality surrounding him, an aura of raw masculinity that made her acutely aware of her own femininity. An awareness was spreading deep within her, accompanied by a curling, pulsing heat.

Oh, this was absurd, she fumed. She'd only just met the man, and to make matters worse, he was in the service. That uniform he wore stood as solid as a concrete wall between them.

"We've gotten off the subject, Mark," she said, lifting her chin. "I suggest we get back to business and you tell me exactly why you're here."

Two

A silence fell over the room, broken only by the crackling of the fire. Eden looked directly at Mark, her eyes radiating determination. She would not be swayed from discovering the reason for his unexpected and unwelcome arrival at the Lazy L.

Mark met her gaze steadily, very aware that he was being pulled in two directions at once. A part of him was seeing only the woman. Blood was pounding heavily in his veins as he reacted to her as a man. The strange desire to protect was there, too, urging him to go to her and gather her into his arms.

But the other part of his being was reminding him he was an Air Force officer on assignment, a highly trained professional whose duty and goal were to complete his mission. There was no room for a beautiful woman who would draw him off course.

Particularly a woman with secrets, like Eden Landry, her very presence at the ranch a mystery.

He knew about deception and how things were not always as they appeared to be. And he was very good at digging out the truth, twisting through the mazes to get where he needed to be.

Never in all his years as an Intelligence officer, had he been swayed by the feminine mystique, the silken web that a woman could spin. And it wasn't going to happen now. Not even if Eden *was* the most beautiful woman he'd ever seen. Not even if she *was* evoking new emotions within him that were foreign and tantalizing. He was there for a specific reason, and he intended to carry on in the proper manner.

"I'm here," he said, still looking directly at her, "to find Captain William Johnson." He leaned forward, resting his elbows on his knees and making a steeple of his fingers. "As you saw on Johnson's registration card, Jim Kenney is listed as the person to notify in case of an emergency. That's because Johnson has no family, and Colonel Kinney is a close friend. As a personal favor to Colonel Kinney, I came to—"

"I don't believe you," she interrupted. "You're indicating a human caring, a personal involvement that simply doesn't exist in the military. One little soldier is lost in the woods and a colonel asks another colonel to go find him? Nice guys, one and all? Sorry, I don't buy it, because I know better. You're just name, rank, and serial numbers, all of you. If you're here to find Captain Johnson, it's because he's important to you somehow, other than a man who's missing in the wilderness. Save your hearts-

and-flowers bit for someone who will believe it. That person, Colonel, is not me."

A flash of anger surged through Mark. He glared at Eden Landry as he stood up, then he moved over to the fire, staring into its flames as he reined in his temper.

Lord, she was bitter toward the military, he thought. He assumed it was because of the deaths of her father and brother. She certainly had no fond memories of her years of growing up as an Army brat either. And she was sharp and had seen through his phony bull as if it were a plate-glass window. He'd better stall, wait and see if the famous Sheriff John Chambers came back in with Bill Johnson in tow.

He turned slowly from the fire to look at her again. "Did you speak with Johnson before he left on that ride? I know you told Colonel Kinney that Johnson had assured you he was an experienced rider, but did you actually see him right before he left?"

"Yes, I did," she said. She seemed surprised at the change of direction in the conversation. "I was in the barn when he was preparing to leave."

"How did he seem to you? Excited about going? Nervous? Quiet?"

"Well, he said something about really needing this break from work and that he was looking forward to getting into the wilderness. He'd done a little fishing in the morning near here, but he planned to ride higher up into the hills."

"Do you remember anything else?" Mark asked, sitting back down in the chair.

"No, that was all. Oh, wait, he did say . . . Well, it was meaningless, just a passing comment."

"What was it?"

"He said, 'Even unicorns are human, you know,' and then he left. It was a strange thing to say, because unicorns aren't human, as everyone knows. I'd forgotten about it until now."

" 'Even unicorns are human,' " Mark repeated. He shook his head and drummed the fingers of one hand on the arm of the chair. "Damn."

Eden leaned toward him. "A nonsensical statement like that is important?"

Before Mark was forced to think of a reply, the sound of an approaching vehicle rumbled outside. Eden stood and started toward the door.

"It's been snowing," she said. "Oh, dear, I hope John has Captain Johnson with him. That's the sheriff's Bronco."

Mark got slowly to his feet. She recognized the sound of the sheriff's four-wheel drive? he wondered. And she called him by his first name? How often was the guy out here? What did a backwoods sheriff look like? No doubt he had a beer belly, swaggered when he walked, and polished his badge in a nightly ritual. He probably wore mirrored sunglasses, too, along with double six-shooters like in a wild west movie.

Eden opened the door, and a blast of cold air swirled through the room. "Come in where it's warm, John," she called. "Oh, no. You're alone. You didn't find him?"

"No," came a voice from the distance.

Damn it, Mark thought.

A moment later a man entered the room and shrugged out of a sheepskin jacket sprinkled with snow. Mark did a quick and thorough inventory of

Sheriff John Chambers. He was thirty, maybe thirty-two, and no beer belly. Six-feet, good build, blond, tanned, looked like he belonged on the beach instead of in the wilds of Montana. He wore khaki pants, a matching shirt that had a small badge on the left breast pocket, and one holstered gun on his right hip. He looked at Mark questioningly.

"Colonel Mark Hampton," he said, extending his hand. "Air Force."

"That's the United States Air Force, John," Eden said, closing the door. "Mark usually makes that extremely clear."

Mark shot her a dark look before shaking hands with John Chambers.

"Sheriff," he said, "Bill Johnson is Captain Johnson of the Air Force. That's why I'm here."

"Come by the fire, John," Eden said. "Would you like some coffee?"

"No, thanks," Chambers said as he walked over to the fireplace. "I can't stay. I just wanted to report to you, Eden. I sent the others back into town with the horses."

"You saw no sign of Johnson at all?" Mark asked.

"Not a thing. The snow covered any tracks he might have left. We sent up flares . . . nothing. I had my men spread out to cover as much ground as possible. We checked the abandoned cabins in the area, but there was no sign that anyone had been in them. Damn, it's frustrating. A man just doesn't disappear off the face of the earth. He must have changed his mind and gone in another direction. Tomorrow we start over, go up the opposite ridge. He's out there somewhere."

So, okay, Mark thought, this was no comic book

sheriff. He knew his stuff. He also spent a lot of time looking at Miss Eden Landry. Sheriff Chambers had apparently forgotten that Colonel Hampton was in the room. Were they lovers, Eden and John? Hell, it was none of his business, and he really didn't care except . . . Except for some ridiculous reason he didn't like the idea one damn bit.

"Sheriff," he said, "I'll be going out with you tomorrow."

"Are you asking or telling?" Eden inquired. "I presume you've backed off from insisting that you take charge of the search?"

Mark's jaw tightened. "You've made your point, Miss Landry. I'm *asking* the sheriff if I may accompany his search party."

"How very polite of you," she said, smiling sweetly.

John Chambers chuckled. "You two hit it off great, I can see. Colonel, what's your interest in this, besides the fact that Bill Johnson is an Air Force captain? We didn't know that, but isn't it unusual to send a colonel to look for a captain in the woods who's on a short leave?"

"It certainly is," Eden said, sitting down. "Colonel Hampton is reluctant to give a reasonable explanation for his presence here."

Chambers grinned at her. "Did it ever occur to you that it's none of your business?"

"I'll be damned," Mark said, smiling. "You and I are going to get along just fine, Sheriff."

Chambers's smile faded. "I have to warn you that it's no picnic up there. Peter Brewer, one of my deputies, got his hat shot off an hour ago. He's still shaking."

"Is he all right?" Eden asked.

"Yeah, he's okay."

"Someone took a shot at him?" Mark asked.

"There are hunters up there, I assume. Thing is, we didn't find evidence of anyone. Nothing. Now it's snowing again. We tracked in the direction the shot came from, but we didn't see a thing."

"You heard only one shot the entire time you were out?" Mark asked.

"Yes, the one that nearly parted Pete's hair. That area is off-limits to hunters. They sneak in there, but they probably spotted us and went on to the other side where they belong."

"One didn't, if he took a potshot at your deputy," Mark said. "Eden, did Johnson have a weapon with him that you know of?"

"There was a Lazy L rifle in the boot of the saddle," she said. "It was still there when the horse came in. If Johnson was carrying a handgun, I wasn't aware of it."

"Well," Chambers said, "whoever fired that shot was quick. He also covered his tracks well, which doesn't make sense. Hunters usually hightail it out of there when they realize there's a sheriff's patrol in the area. This one took the time to make sure he couldn't be followed. Anyway, the bottom line is, we have no idea where Bill Johnson is at the moment. I hope he has as much wilderness survival training as he claimed. It's damn cold up there, and getting colder."

"According to his file," Mark said, "he's very well trained in wilderness survival. I've never met him, though I've seen his picture."

"Well, you're welcome to join us at dawn," Chambers said. "I'll come by for you, then we'll drive up to where my men unload the horses. Dress warm, Colonel."

"Mark."

"Okay, Mark. I'll be glad to have another pair of eyes and ears up there. Do remember that I'm running this show."

"No problem."

"Well, do tell," Eden said. Mark slid her another glare.

Chambers laughed. "Eden is not crazy about uniforms, Mark," he said, starting toward the door.

"*You* wear one," Mark said.

"True," he said, shrugging into his jacket. "But I don't salute anyone, nor do I follow orders other than my own. Big difference there. Eden, don't poison or shoot Mark tonight, will you? I need all the help I can get finding that lost soldier."

"Very funny," Eden muttered.

The sheriff reached in his pockets for his gloves. "What . . . Oh, yeah, I forgot about this." He pulled something from one pocket. "Just a piece of junk, I guess."

Mark crossed the room. "What is it?"

Chambers extended his hand. "A two-inch unicorn, made out of metal. Looks like the kind of thing that sits on a shelf with a collection or something. Some kid probably lost it up there."

"Could I see it?" Mark asked.

"Sure," the sheriff said, handing it to him.

Mark examined the small figurine. "Do you remember where you were up there where you found it?"

"Yes."

"Could you show me on a map in the morning?"

"Yes, but we covered that whole area inch by inch. In fact, we were coming back through that way when Pete had to dodge the bullet. Why the interest in that toy?"

"Bill Johnson said something about—" Eden started.

"Sheriff . . . John"—Mark interrupted—"I'll tell you what I can, when I can. Meanwhile, I'd appreciate your cooperation. I'd like to see where you found this unicorn. Do your men know you found it?"

"No. They were spread out by then. I put it in my pocket and forgot about it."

"Please don't mention it to anyone. That goes for you, too, Eden. I'll keep this for now, if you don't mind." He slipped it into his pocket.

"Whatever you say," Chambers said. "I'll see you in the morning. I assume you're trained for search and rescue, Mark, or they wouldn't have sent you here."

"I'm trained."

"Fair enough. I'll bring an extra horse along."

"Make that two extra horses," Eden said. "I'm going back out with you tomorrow. We can use Lazy L horses if you like."

"There's no reason for you to go, Eden," Mark said. "You heard John. There are some trigger-happy hunters out there."

"There's also a lost man out there. I'm going."

"Look, Eden, just stay here."

"Save your breath, Colonel," Chambers said, smiling as he opened the door. "Once she's made up her mind, that's it. You'll be talking to the wind. I'll have my men take our horses up, Eden. We'll use Lazy L mounts later if we need them. See you both at dawn."

"Wait a minute," Eden said. "Mark won't be here. He's staying in town tonight."

"Wrong," Mark said. "See you in the morning, John."

"Yep," Chambers said. He waved as he left. Mark closed the door behind him.

"Nice guy," he said, turning to Eden. He gave her his best hundred-watt smile. "I like your John. Seems to know his stuff too."

She crossed her arms and tapped one foot. "He is not *my* John," she said tightly. "Yes, he's a very good sheriff, and, no, you are not staying at the Lazy L tonight. Only four of the cabins are winterized, and they're being used by hunters."

He glanced around. "This is a big house. Surely you have a spare bedroom."

"This is my home, Colonel. Guests of the Lazy L don't stay under this roof."

"Oh. Well, I'll bunk in Bill's cabin."

"Someone else is using it. Two hunters had reservations for it, and I had to remove Captain Johnson's things and put them in a storage shed. I hated to touch his personal belongings, but I had no choice. So, as you can see, there's no room at the inn. You'll have to go into town."

"No can do. This is where my superior officer expects to reach me. I have to be available." That was a crock, Mark thought. A simple call would inform the general of a motel phone number. But for some unknown reason Mark wanted to stay right there at the Lazy L, close to Eden Landry. "I won't be in your way. With any luck, we'll find Bill Johnson tomorrow, then he and I will be gone."

"But . . ."

"Look, I'll bring my things in and change my clothes. Then I'll need to go through his possessions. I have to make some calls later too. I'll be so busy, you won't even know I'm here."

Ha! Eden thought. Mark Hampton was so *there* it was incredible. The essence of the man seemed to fill the room to overflowing. She'd always considered John Chambers a rugged individual who could handle himself well in any given situation. Yet while the two men had been together, Mark had overshadowed John with some intangible power, an indefinable something that she couldn't quite put a name to except to call it "male," in capital letters. Not know that Mark Hampton was there? What a joke.

"Okay, then?" he asked, raising his hands in a gesture of peace. "I can stay here tonight?"

"I suppose so." She paused. "What's all this business about the unicorn?"

Mark took the tiny figurine from his pocket and looked at it. "I'll tell you when I can. Hopefully, after I make those phone calls. I'd like to change and see Bill's things right away."

"All right. Do you always get your own way like this?"

He looked directly into her eyes, and his voice was low when he spoke. "Usually. Sometimes it's because I outrank someone else. And other times . . . Well, it depends on how badly I want what I'm after."

They were no longer discussing Air Force matters, Eden realized. The warm flutter in her stomach and the sudden racing of her heart told her in no uncertain terms that Mark was talking about a man wanting a woman. About him wanting her. She could see it in his gray eyes, a raw desire that he was making no attempt to disguise. No! Mark Hampton might be used to getting what he wanted from women, but not this time.

"You're old enough to know," she said, lifting her chin, "that you can't always have what you want."

"I'm also old enough to know that if it's worth having, it's worth fighting for. I don't like to lose."

"Do you fight fair?" she asked, aware of the breathlessness in her voice.

"Not always." He looked at her for another long moment, then turned toward the door. "I'll bring my things in."

Eden blinked as though coming out of a trance. She shivered, but not from the cold air that swept over her when Mark opened the door.

He was jangling her, she thought angrily. She used to be an expert at dealing with men like Mark Hampton. When she'd lived in New York, she'd been able to hold her own against anything in pants. Even on the ranch, she'd had no difficulty sidestepping male guests who were coming on too strong. She was not accustomed to feeling vulnerable and off balance because of a man. Mark Hampton was doing tricky things to her mind, and her body was going nuts. Well, enough of this nonsense. Eden Landry was back in control!

Half an hour later, Eden unlocked the door to a small shed and stepped inside. Mark was right behind her.

"Those are Captain Johnson's things," she said as she turned on the light. "There, in that one suitcase. This shed is heated, so you won't be uncomfortable. I'll leave you to do whatever you need to do."

"No," he said. "I'll need a witness since I'm going through his personal property." That wasn't true, he thought. He had authority to do this under the circumstances. But an Eden close to him was much better than an Eden going back up to the house. "It won't take me long."

"Fine," she said, forcefully closing the door. "Do I salute now or later?" Darn the man. Why was he so gorgeous? He also seemed to be drawing the oxygen from within this tiny shed, the very air from her lungs. In faded jeans, boots, gray flannel shirt, and a heavy, fleece-lined Air Force jacket, he was massive, masculine, and magnificent. And her heart was doing its tap dance again. She'd bet he'd worn that shirt because he knew it matched his eyes and did wonderful things for his dark hair with its smattering of silver. The rat.

Mark hunkered down in front of the suitcase and snapped it open. He removed the contents, then examined the empty case for hidden chambers, a false bottom, and loose linings. Nothing. He began to replace the personal articles one by one. There was nothing unusual about what Bill Johnson had packed for a weekend in rough, cold terrain. There were heavy shirts, socks, an extra pair of jeans, underwear.

He picked up a leather case and unzipped it, finding, as he'd expected, shaving gear, a brush, and a comb. He removed the articles and slid his hand inside the now empty case.

"Bingo," he said.

"What is it?" Eden asked.

"There's something under the side lining."

She moved closer and dropped to her knees beside him.

Oh, Lord, he thought, as he worked to free the lining, Eden smelled so good, like fresh air, soap, and a light, flowery perfume. Maybe it was the Eden perfume he'd seen in the stores. He wanted to forget the damn case, just drop it to the floor, and turn his head and capture Eden's lips with his own. He'd sink his fingers into that lush, dark auburn hair of hers to hold her head steady while he savored her taste. He'd explore every crevice of her mouth and stroke her tongue with his. Oh, yes, he wanted to kiss her, wanted to feel her passion, not as anger but as flaming desire.

Heat shot through him, and he cleared his throat, telling himself to concentrate on working the lining of the case free. It came loose at the top, and he inched his fingers inside, then closed them around a hard object.

"Did you get it?" she asked.

He removed his hand and opened it palm up so she could see.

"Oh," she gasped. "It's another unicorn, exactly like the one John found."

"Yeah," Mark said gruffly. "Here, hold it while I put this stuff away."

He dropped the unicorn into her hand. She stood up, examining the tiny metal statue as Mark replaced Bill's possessions. He snapped the suitcase closed, slapped his hands onto his thighs, and pushed himself to his feet.

"Mark," she said, still looking at the unicorn, "this one's sterling silver and exquisitely made. It's dark like the other one because it's tarnished. The details are so clear when you look close. It certainly isn't a child's toy."

He unzipped a side pocket of his jacket and took out the unicorn John Chambers had given him. He turned it in his fingers, looking at it closely.

"This one is tarnished sterling too," he said. "Do you have any silver polish at the house?"

"Yes."

She looked up at him at the exact moment he turned to gaze at her. Their eyes met, held. A pulsing heat seemed to weave back and forth between them, curling within them.

Run! Eden told herself, but she didn't move. Oh, Lord, what was happening here? What strange spell was Mark Hampton casting over her? She wanted him to kiss her. Now! Oh, please, yes, right now.

No! Her sensible side shouted. This man was dangerous to the tranquil existence she'd worked so hard to find and protect. She didn't want him here. She didn't want to feel stirrings she'd put on hold so long ago. No!

One kiss, a little voice within her whispered. Just one.

He had to kiss her, Mark thought. It was no longer up for thought. He ached for the feel of her lips beneath his.

His gaze never leaving hers, he slipped the unicorn back into his pocket and lifted his hand to the nape of her neck. Slowly, so slowly, he bent his head to seek her mouth, anticipation causing a tight coil of desire to throb deep and low within him.

"Eden," he said, his voice raspy.

Her name was a soft puff of air against her lips,

and Eden felt a trembling within her as she waited. In less than a heartbeat, Mark's lips would claim hers. Her cheeks flushed, and her lips parted slightly in invitation.

He kissed her.

Oh, yes, he thought.

At last, she thought.

The kiss was gentle, sensual, teasing at first. Then Mark slipped his tongue inside her mouth and a low groan rumbled up from his chest. He shifted to bring her to him, to nestle her as close as their bulky jackets would allow. He circled her back with his arm, his other hand still at her nape. Her arms floated to entwine around his neck.

The kiss became hungry, urgent, as they savored the taste and feel of each other. They sampled each other's sweetness and wanted more. Their tongues dueled in a rhythmic motion that fanned passions to a fever pitch. Their breathing was rough, echoing in the small shed.

Enough, Hampton! Mark screamed at himself. He was slipping over the edge, losing control. This never happened to him, not to him. His body and his mind were under his command . . . always. But, oh, Lord, how he wanted this woman. No! He had to stop. Right now!

He tore his lips from Eden's and stepped back so suddenly that she was forced to drop her arms from his neck. She opened her eyes and staggered slightly as a wave of dizziness assaulted her. His fists curled tightly at his sides, Mark started up at the ceiling for a long moment, drawing in deep breaths, as he thrust down his passion.

Eden pressed trembling fingers to her kiss-swollen

lips, her eyes widening in horror. Dear heaven, what had she done?

Mark gazed at her again. "Oh, damn," he said, his voice still husky with desire. "Don't look so frightened, as though you think I'm going to throw you on the floor and ravish you. We shared that kiss, Eden. We both wanted it."

"Yes," she whispered. "Yes, I wanted you to kiss me. I admit that, Mark, but it isn't going to happen again."

A slow grin crept onto his face. "It isn't?"

"No," she said, amazed that her voice was now at a normal level.

He shrugged his massive shoulders. "Okay."

She placed her hand on his arm. "I mean it. I don't do things like this. I realize I just did, but I don't. Oh, damn, that didn't make sense."

He chuckled, then instantly wiped the smile from his face. He looked at her with an innocent expression, as if what she was saying was extremely fascinating.

"You may have gotten the wrong impression of me," she rushed on. "I don't leap into the arms of men I don't know and . . . What I'm saying is, Colonel Hampton, there will be no more kisses, or anything else. Nothing."

"Oh," he said, nodding slowly. "I see."

She glared at him. "I hope you do. I apologize for my behavior."

He couldn't contain his laughter. "You apologize for your behavior? You sound like something out of the Victorian age."

"Don't you laugh at me, Mark Hampton." She spun around and marched to the door.

He covered the space with two long strides and slammed his hand flat against the door just above her head, blocking her exit. She turned toward him, her eyes sparkling with anger.

"Move your big paw and let me out of here," she said.

"No," he said, inching closer to her.

She backed up and thudded against the door, scowling at him. He slid his hand down to the side of her head, then placed his other hand on the other side. He moved nearer, trapping her, yet not touching her body with any part of his.

"I'm warning you . . ." she said, damning the trembling she heard in her voice and felt in her knees.

"You can apologize from here to Sunday for your behavior," he said, his voice low and rumbly, "but you'll never convince me you didn't want and enjoy that kiss as much as I did."

"I admitted that."

"Then what's the problem? We didn't do anything wrong. And there wouldn't be anything wrong with me kissing you again."

"Yes, there would because . . . Forget that. You're not going to kiss me again. I've made that very clear."

"Why would it be wrong, Eden?" he asked. His voice seemed to drop an octave. "Because you wanted more than a kiss? You wanted me? I wanted you, you know." He brushed his lips over hers and she shivered. "I still want you. My body is aching for you, Eden Landry." He kissed one side of her mouth, then the other. "Did you feel it, Eden? The heat, the desire, burning in me, in you, in us together?"

"No," she whispered.

"What are you afraid of? Me? I won't hurt you. What kind of man do you think I am? I would never take more from you than you were willing to give."

"I don't intend," she said forcefully, "to give you anything."

"And that kiss?"

"Was a mistake. Now, let me out of this shed, Colonel."

"Not yet." He moved one hand to her neck, lightly tracing the line of her jaw with his thumb. "I want to make sure I have all my facts straight. You just shared a kiss with me that was incredible. A kiss we both wanted, needed to have. You responded to me totally, and Lord knows I reacted to you. That kiss was magic, Eden, and very, very special. A mistake? No. No way. A beginning."

"No."

"Which brings me back to my question. What are you afraid of?"

"Nothing.

"Why are you here on this ranch in the middle of nowhere? What are you hiding from? Why won't you admit that you wanted me as much as I wanted you?"

"Stop it," she said, pushing against his chest. She immediately discovered it was like trying to move a brick wall. "I don't want to hear one more word of your blithering. We shared a kiss, there will be no more, that's it. Don't touch me again, Mark."

He slowly straightened and stepped back, his face expressionless.

"Understand?" she asked. "Is it finally clear?"

"I heard you, Eden. Every word. Where's the unicorn you had in your hand?"

"What? Oh, I dropped it, I guess. Yes, it's there on the floor."

Mark picked it up and took the other one from his pocket. "I want to clean these up."

"Yes, all right, but . . ."

He looked at her again. "But?"

"You said you heard what I said, but do you understand? There will be no repeat performance of what happened in this shed."

He moved around her and opened the door. Snow and frigid air swirled inside.

"Boy, it's really doing its thing out here." He stepped out of the shed, then glanced back at her. "Coming?"

She came, shut the door with more force than necessary, and locked it. Mark started in the direction of the house, and she had to hurry to catch up with him.

"Mark," she yelled over the howling wind, "you didn't answer me."

"I didn't?" he asked. "You want me to comment on your wanting no more of what took place in that shed?"

"Well, yes," she said, nearly running to stay beside him.

"Okay. My comment is"—he flashed her a dazzling smile—"bull."

She stopped dead in her tracks. "What?"

He kept walking. "You heard me," he shouted back. "You do want more, Eden Landry. It all depends on whether or not you have enough courage to admit it to yourself. Do *you* understand? The word is 'bull.' "

"Despicable," she muttered, stomping after him. "And arrogant, cocky, rude."

And right, she thought glumly. Her body was still throbbing with hot desire. She could recall the taste, the aroma, the feel of Mark so clearly, it was as if he were still holding her.

Oh, yes, she had wanted more when he'd kissed her, when he'd pressed her against his hard body. She'd wanted to make love with Mark Hampton. And now? If he turned around and came back to her, drew her close and covered her lips with his, she'd probably melt in his arms and shout "Hooray!" Darn, darn, and damn, what was this man doing to her? And to top it off, the bum knew she'd dissolve into a willing heap if he touched her.

"The louse," she said, as he entered the house up ahead. "Bull, is it?" Well, she had news for strut-his-stuff Colonel Hampton. She had no intention of falling prey to his masculine magnetism again. The kiss was a no-big-deal forgotten occurrence as of that very moment. And if he tried his seduction routine again, she'd punch him right in his gorgeous nose!

Three

Eden certainly wasn't expecting Mark to have a "strictly business" attitude when she entered the house. He had hung his snow-covered jacket in the mud room, and she found him in the kitchen, leaning against a counter. His long legs were crossed at the ankle, and he was staring at the two small unicorns in his hand.

He glanced up when she came in. "Would you mind getting me the silver polish, please?" he asked.

"Silver polish," she repeated, turning toward the pantry. Silver polish? They'd just had a screamer in the snow about that mind-boggling kiss, and the man was now thinking about silver polish?

Was that insulting? she asked herself, as she searched the pantry shelf. Had he already dusted off what had transpired between them? Well! The nerve. Yes, that was definitely insulting.

She sighed. And she wasn't making a bit of sense.

She'd demanded that Mark leave her alone, never touch her again. Yet now that he was being polite, concentrating on why he'd really come to the Lazy L, she was feeling insulted? She must be losing her mind.

She came back into the kitchen with the silver polish and a soft dust-rag. "Have you ever used this stuff before?" she asked.

"No."

"Would you like me to do it?"

"Sure, if you wouldn't mind." He dropped the unicorns into her hand but didn't meet her gaze.

"It won't take long. Help yourself to the coffee," she said. "I'll have some when I'm finished here."

Mark pushed himself away from the counter and walked over to the stove. She watched him from beneath her lashes, her gaze lingering on his wide shoulders and the way his jeans hugged his narrow hips and muscled thighs. She felt her pulse skitter, and quickly turned to the sink and the project of cleaning the tarnished unicorns.

Mark sipped his coffee and studied Eden from behind, his gaze skimming over her silky hair, her back, then all the way down to her long, long legs.

He had, he admitted, come on a bit strong by not letting Eden leave the shed. But, dammit, she'd been ready to write that kiss off, forget it ever happened. He hadn't liked that. That kiss had been sensational and very special, magical, just as he'd said. Lord, how he'd wanted her. He had nearly lost control of himself. He couldn't, wouldn't, let her just chalk it up and forget it. Something important had happened between them in that shed, and he wanted to know what it all meant.

Easy, Hampton, he told himself. He hadn't stayed alive this long in the places he'd been and carrying out the assignments he'd had, by rushing in without thinking things through. The same had to be true for Eden Landry. Slow and easy. His famous self-control. Patience. One step at a time.

He'd never had to apply his training as an Intelligence officer to figuring out a woman, but how tough could it be? A puzzle was a puzzle. The fact that this one was a delectable, beautiful woman who was turning him inside out like no woman ever had was beside the point. He wanted to make love with Eden, and she wanted him. Pure and simple. He'd find Bill Johnson and unravel the puzzle that was Eden in the process. Fine. Piece of cake.

He continued to sip his coffee, a very smug, very male expression on his face.

Eden turned on the warm water and rinsed the white cream off the unicorns.

"These are absolutely lovely," she said. "Mark, get that dish towel, will you?"

He handed her the towel and stood next to her as she dried the tiny statues.

"There," she said, giving him one. "Look at the detail on these. I think they're expensive, probably custom-made. See the loop on the unicorn's back? They're meant to be worn on a necklace or a charm bracelet."

"Two-inch charms?" he said, turning the unicorn over in his hand. "It would be a heavy bracelet."

"It depends on the woman's taste, and perhaps her own size. One wouldn't be too big as a necklace on a long chain. But two? They'd just lie on top of each other and wouldn't be very attractive. Maybe they sat on a shelf like John said."

"Then why the loops?" Mark asked, frowning. "Especially if they're custom-made. I guess they could be attached to a linked chain at intervals so they wouldn't bang against each other. I really don't know that much about jewelry." He looked at the bottom of the figure. "Hey, what's this? There's a very small letter *A* on one of the hooves."

Eden turned over the one she held. "And there's an *N* here. See? Do you think that's the initial of the person who made them? No, that doesn't add up. They were made by the same person, I'd bet on it. Why would he use two different initials as his trademark, even if both do represent his name? He'd want to be known for the quality of his work, not confuse the issue by bouncing back and forth between his first name and last. I think maybe . . . Well . . ."

He smiled at her. "Don't stop now, you're doing great. You'll have my job at the rate you're going."

"Your job, whatever it is, you can keep," she said, matching his smile. "Okay, I think the initials belong to the person these were made for. I also think maybe they aren't initials, but part of a name, a whole name. Yes, it would make a very heavy, large charm bracelet, but that's where I'm putting my nickel bet."

Mark laughed. "A nickel? You don't have much faith in your theory, Miss Landry."

"Due to the fact, Colonel Hampton, that I have no idea what I'm talking about. You have just heard the full extent of my Perry Mason repertoire. You, I take it, are trained to figure out these things."

He nodded. "Supposedly. Truth is, your analysis is better than mine."

"Oh? What's yours?"

"I don't have one at the moment," he said, grinning.

She really wished he wouldn't smile at her like that, she thought. It caused funny little sensations within her, hot sensations. She could handle being near him better when he was arrogant.

"Well, here you go," she said, dropping her unicorn into his hand. "I'll clean up this mess from the polish."

"May I use your phone?" he asked. "The government will pay for the calls."

"My taxes, you mean. There's a phone in the library off the living room. You'll have privacy there." She glanced out the window over the sink. "Oh, Mark, look at the snow. I'll turn on the radio for a weather report. I hate to think of Bill Johnson being lost in that storm. I hope he's in one of the abandoned cabins John didn't get to yet. He has to be in some kind of shelter to survive this."

"He's trained, remember?" Mark said. "You'd be surprised what a man can survive. Sometimes the man himself is surprised he made it."

She looked up at him quickly. "You sound as though you're speaking from experience."

He shrugged. "Old news. I'll use the phone."

She watched as he left the kitchen. What had he been through in the past? she wondered. There was a Purple Heart on his dress uniform, along with all his other ribbons and medals. Why didn't he fly for the Air Force anymore? Did it have to do with the wound he'd sustained to earn the Purple Heart? How difficult and frustrating it would be for a pilot if he could no longer fly his beloved planes. And how terrible for Mark if it were true. Magnificent Mark.

The women must flock after him like panting puppies, she mused. Was there a special woman waiting for him? Oh, forget it, she told herself. She didn't care. But . . .

"Clean up this mess, Eden," she said, turning back to the sink, "and tell your brain to give it a rest."

The library was a man's room, Mark thought. The wood furniture was massive and dark. The large desk, hand carved across the front, had a butter-soft leather chair behind it. One wall had floor-to-ceiling shelves filled with books, and heavy, dark drapes were closed over the windows. Logs had been laid in the fireplace, ready to come alive with warming flames, and a wide-screen television set stood next to it.

He closed the door and made his way forward in the dimness to snap on the lamp on the desk. The light sent just enough luminescence over the room to give it a welcoming glow.

He sighed as he sank into the plush, leather chair. This would be a man's haven, he thought, the room he'd use to unwind, relax, gather his thoughts. He'd tend to business at the desk, then light the fire and settle in to watch a football game. The children, of course, would always be welcome, would never feel intimidated. They'd come to him with their good news and bad, their joys and sorrows, and he'd listen to every word.

Then later, after the kids were asleep, his wife would nestle close to him on the sofa in front of the fire, and they'd talk, or just be silent. The firelight would flicker over Eden's auburn hair, accentuating the highlights, and her beautiful eyes would grow smoky with desire. He'd pull her close and—

Mark stiffened in the chair. "What?" he said aloud. Where was all this nonsense coming from? He had never in his life spun a fantasy about being married and having children.

And, dammit, he fumed, Eden had been in that mind game. She was the wife. The children were theirs. Lord, this was nuts. One kiss and he was daydreaming about marrying the woman? What in the hell was the matter with him? And even more, what was Eden Landry doing to his sanity? Wanting her in his bed was one thing, but envisioning her as his wife and the mother of his children was another. Crazy, that's what it was. Whatever strange things Eden was managing to do to his well-ordered mind, she'd better just knock it off.

"Damn right," he said gruffly, and reached for the telephone.

Like metal slivers pulled to a magnet, his glance slid once more to the cold hearth and the sofa in front of it. He envisioned again the fire burning and Eden tucked close to his side, then with an earthy expletive he snapped his attention back to the telephone.

After giving the operator his credit card number and the number of the new private line into General Meyers's office, he leaned back in the chair and waited for the call to go through. There was a great deal of static on the line, and the operator informed him she would place the call again, hoping for clearer transmission.

Mark's gaze fell on a framed picture on the corner

of the desk. It was a color photograph of a family gathered in front of a lake. A tall blond man stood next to a woman who had a remarkable resemblance to Eden, from her auburn hair to her long legs. She held a baby in her arms, and a blond boy about ten or eleven years old stood in front of the man.

This was Eden's family, Mark realized. They were in casual clothes, as if on vacation, and they were all smiling, even the chubby baby. Eden was the baby, he was sure of it. And that would be the father and brother, now dead. What had happened to her mother?

"I'm still working to connect your call, sir," the operator said. "We have lines down from this storm."

"I'll wait," he said. "Do the best you can. The wind is really howling out there."

"Yes, sir. This storm was unexpected, came in with a new weather front. I'll try to patch through."

"Thank you."

Mark set the unicorns in front of him, and the mythical creatures gleamed in the lamp light. He frowned at them, knowing that they had complicated the simple situation of a man lost in the woods.

His attention was drawn to another object on the desk, and he leaned closer for a better look. It was a glass cube about four inches on each side, and encased in the cube was a delicate crystal butterfly perched on a crystal flower. The butterfly's wings were raised as though it were ready to fly quickly away should anything frighten it.

It didn't have to worry, he thought absently. It was protected by walls so nothing could get to it. "Keep your wings on, honey," he said to the butterfly, and ran one fingertip across the top of the glass cube.

"I can place your call now, sir," the operator said.

"What?" he said, momentarily forgetting he still had the receiver pressed to his ear. "Good. Thanks."

There was more crackling on the line, then the sound of a ringing telephone.

"Meyers," a deep voice said.

"Mark."

"We've been waiting to hear from you, Mark. Kinney is sitting right here. Have you found Johnson?"

"No. There's no trace of him yet, General."

"Damn."

"General, what do you have for me on the people here?" Mark rested his elbows on the desk.

"Not much. They're private citizens with driver's licenses, social security numbers. No one has any kind of police record. There's a Fred and Jane Sawyer, who work there full-time. The rest are part-time help from the area. Clean as a whistle."

"And Eden Landry?" Mark asked, feeling a sudden knot in his stomach.

"Unusual, but not illegal. She was a high-fashion model who dropped out of the business five years ago. Her Eden products are still selling like hotcakes, and her agent sees to her endorsement on new fashions each season. She's a very wealthy woman and has a steady incoming flow of cash with no end in sight."

"Family?"

"Let's see. Okay, here it is. Mother died of cancer twenty years ago. Father was career Army, died of a heart attack in Vietnam. Brother was Army infantry. Wounded in Vietnam. Died three years ago."

"Of what?" Mark asked, frowning.

"The report on him is from the Veterans Administration. Not a lot here. Just says Phillip Landry Junior died of complications from injuries sustained during tour of duty in Vietnam. Both Landry men were buried at Arlington with full military honors."

"And Eden was given the folded flags," Mark muttered under his breath.

"What?"

"Nothing. There's a bunch of years in there, General, between when Phillip Junior was wounded and when he died of those injuries. Where was he in the meantime?"

"I don't know, but I can find out if you think it's important."

"No, forget it. The man is dead. General, who named Kinney's team Project Unicorn?"

"I'll ask him." There was a murmur of voices, then the general came back on the line. "Jim said Johnson named it."

"Hell." Mark slouched back in the chair. "I was afraid of that. A two-inch sterling silver unicorn was found on the trail in the woods. I found another concealed in the lining of Bill's shaving kit."

"What the hell does that mean?"

"I don't know, but I don't like it. A deputy was shot at during the search. The sheriff here, who's no dope, would like to chalk it up to a hunter, but he's questioning it because the triggerman covered his tracks. Did you check out Sheriff John Chambers?"

"Yep. Local boy. Went to college, came home. That's it. You're surrounded by clean-living citizens, Mark. Do you think something fishy is going on with Johnson?"

"I'm not thrilled with how it's adding up so far, that's for sure. These unicorns mean something, I'd bet on it. Why did he carry one and hide the other? The security clearance files on the Project Unicorn team are thin, very sloppy work."

"Which is why that particular officer is soaking up Florida sun in early retirement. He was an all-around screwup. They're doing a helluva good job, though, that Unicorn team."

"Well, I need more information on Johnson than what is in his file. He says no family. What about a woman? There are initials on the bottom of the unicorns too. An *N* on one and an *A* on the other. I don't think it's the artist's trademark because they look custom-made by the same person. The artist would use the same initial consistently. I'm leaning toward it being the initials of a woman, or part of her name. There are loops on the unicorns for them to be attached to a charm bracelet or a necklace."

"And one was carefully concealed?"

"Yes."

"Not good."

"I don't have any idea where all this is leading, but I have a feeling it's a lot more than a guy lost in the woods. Will you see what you can dig up on Johnson's personal life?"

"I'll get right on it, Mark."

"General, Chambers found the unicorn on the trail, and Eden Landry was with me when I discovered the other one. I'm going to have to trust them, probably fill them in a bit more."

"It's your baby, Mark. Go with whatever feels right."

"Thank you, sir. There's a wild snowstorm out there right now. We plan to start searching again at dawn, but we'd have to have better weather than this to see farther than our noses. I have a feeling that if something doesn't break soon, Chambers will want to call in the National Guard."

"No, absolutely not," General Meyers said. "We'll fly in our own security-cleared rescue team if we have to. Tell only the minimum to the locals you trust, Mark. We're sitting on a powder keg with this mess. The President is none too pleased. My orders are to report to him every time I hear from you. Damn, Mark, where do you suppose Johnson is?"

"I wish I knew," he said, picking up one of the unicorns.

"Mark?"

"Yes, sir?"

"Find him."

Mark rolled his eyes. "Yes, sir. I understand."

"I'll get back to you when I have more on Johnson's personal life. You call me the minute you have anything, no matter how small."

"Yes, sir."

"Good-bye, Colonel."

"Good-bye, General."

Mark slowly hung up the phone, then picked up the other unicorn. He stared at both silver statues, then shook his head and dropped them into his shirt pocket. He stood up, shoved his hands into his back pockets, and wandered around the room, sifting through his mind the little he knew about Bill Johnson's disappearance.

The bottom line was, he had to find Johnson. And if Johnson didn't want to be found? If he'd sold what was in his genius brain to the highest bidder? What then? Or what if he had been snatched? That meant a leak in Project Unicorn. Someone else could have been bought and divulged the information that

Johnson had the entire computer program in his head. If that was the case, how had they lured him out of Washington and to the Lazy L at exactly the right moment? Damn, it was a complicated puzzle. And he had to solve it before national security was put at more risk.

He walked over to the fireplace, then turned to look at the sofa. He saw again in his mind's eye the scenario he had created earlier, Eden sitting next to him there, smiling up at him. Heat rocketed through his body as he relived that kiss in the shed.

He even liked the sound of her name, he mused. It was unique, just like the woman herself. What in heaven's name was she doing on a ranch in the middle of Montana? It had been five years since she'd walked away from her life of glamour. Why? Everywhere he turned there were unanswered questions.

A scratching noise at the door brought Mark back to the present and away from the jumbled maze in his mind. He strode to the door and opened it, then quickly moved back as an enormous black and silver German shepherd bounded into the room, tail wagging.

Mark smiled. "Well, hello, dog." He extended his hand for the animal's inspection. "Where did you come from?"

The dog sniffed Mark's hand, licked it with his large tongue, then sat down, his tail thumping on the floor.

"Samson!" Eden called. "Where are you?"

Mark stepped out into the hall. "If you're looking for a horse masquerading as a dog, he's in here."

"Samson, you don't mind me at all," she said,

laughing. She entered the library and scratched the wiggling dog behind the ears. "He's just a puppy really. He's been following Jane and Fred around all day. They spoil him rotten."

"Jane and Fred?"

"Jane and Fred Sawyer. They look after things. They live in that large cabin down by the barn. Fred tends to the ranch, the horses, all that. Jane takes care of the cabins. When there's extra work to be done, they hire local boys. I don't know what I'd do without them."

"What is your role here on the Lazy L?" Mark asked, leaning his shoulder against the wall.

"I do all the books, the ordering of supplies, take care of advertising and reservations. There's an unbelievable amount of paperwork involved in running a place like this."

"Are you happy here, Eden?" he asked quietly.

She switched her gaze from Samson to him. "Happy? That's a rather subjective term. I'm . . . content, at peace. Happiness is hard to define. It's a quicksilver entity that is here, then gone."

"You've lost me."

"Well, suppose it's your birthday and your friends give you a surprise party. It's wonderful, very touching, and you say, 'Oh, I'm so happy.' The next day you have lovely memories of the party, but you don't have that happy-high you had when it took place. So, like I say, happiness is here, then gone. But contentment? A feeling of peacefulness? Those are more stable."

He nodded. "I see. I take it you were no longer content in your glamorous world in New York?"

"I didn't really think about it. I just did what I was

supposed to do. Then . . . Well, as I said before, it's a long story."

"I have plenty of time to listen."

She gazed at him for a long moment. "I'll start supper," she said, walking toward the door.

"Eden."

His low voice held the command of authority. She stopped, but she didn't look at him.

"Yes?"

"Why are you here?"

Her head snapped around. "I live and work here, Colonel," she said tightly.

"Why?"

"That's none of your business. I lived in New York, and now I live in Montana. Why do you keep pushing at me like this?"

Mark straightened away from the wall. "Because I need answers, a lot of them, in a very complicated and potentially dangerous situation. You're an intelligent woman. I'm sure you've figured out that those unicorns and where they were found aren't exactly run-of-the-mill. I need your help, I need to trust you, but I have to know who you are, why you're here."

"I don't care whether you trust me or not," she said, striding out of the room.

"Don't you?"

She spun around and came back into the library. "No. I . . ." She paused, then threw up her hands. "Yes, I care. I haven't done anything wrong, I have no secrets. I'm a private person, that's all, and there are things I don't want to discuss because they're just too painful." She crossed the room to the desk and stood with her back to him. "I'll do everything I can to help you find Bill Johnson, but my personal life has nothing to do with the fact that he's missing. You can believe that, or not. It's entirely up to you."

He did believe her, Mark realized, and he did trust her. He now knew he wanted her to trust *him* enough to share herself with him. She said she had no secrets, but she did. Not anything connected with Bill Johnson, but the answers to who Eden Landry, the person, was. He wanted to know everything about her, big, small, important, mundane. Why had she walked—or run—away from her life in New York? What was her favorite color? Had she ever been in love? Did she like green beans? All and everything . . . he needed to know.

He walked across the room to stand behind her. She had picked up the glass cube containing the crystal butterfly and was staring down at it.

"All right, Eden, I'll trust you," he said. "I believe you aren't involved in this mess with Bill Johnson."

"Thank you," she said softly.

"I just wish *you* trusted *me*."

"I . . ."

"You're like that butterfly," he went on. "You're beautiful . . . and fragile. And you've surrounded yourself with walls. I can see you, you can see me, but no one can touch you, not really. Just like that butterfly."

She set the glass cube back on the desk and turned to look at him. "The butterfly is safe. It can't be hurt or harmed in there."

He gazed directly into her eyes. "But isn't the butterfly lonely behind those walls?"

"No," she whispered.

"Are you sure?" He lifted his hands to frame her

face. "Are you very sure the butterfly isn't lonely, Eden?"

His lips claimed hers, and she responded instantly. Suspended in pleasure, she savored the taste, the feel, the strength of Mark. His heat invaded her body, consumed her, and she sank her fingers into his thick night-black hair. All rational thought fled as she met his tongue with her own.

It was all their first kiss had been . . . and more. Much more. It was passion rising and hearts racing. It was desire pulsing low, and heavy and hot in one body taut with muscles and in one body soft and gently curved.

"Eden," Mark murmured, his lips still close to hers. "Oh, Eden, what are you doing to me?"

"Only—only what you're doing to me." She started to pull away.

"No, don't go. I'm not going to hurt you."

"There are different kinds of hurt, Mark."

"I know that. I have no intention of hurting you in any way. Eden, don't keep me on the outside of those protective walls of yours. I want to know who you are, what you think. What books you read, the music you like, everything. I want you to come to trust me enough to share your secrets with me, even though you claim you don't have any. And I want to make love with you."

She moved back from him. "That's quite a list of wants," she said, staring down at Samson flopped on the floor.

"I suppose it is. But none of them are unreasonable. Eden, don't you want to know what this is that's happening between us?"

She looked up at him. "Yes. No. What's the point,

Mark? Surely you haven't forgotten your spiffy blue uniform. You'll find Bill Johnson and return to a life of saluting and following orders and forget I ever existed. No, thank you. I don't want to pursue what's happening between us any further. I spent my life waving good-bye to a man in uniform. I'll never cry that kind of tears again."

"Your father was the one who kept leaving you?"

"Yes, after my mother had died." Tears filled her eyes and spilled onto her cheeks. "And then my brother. He broke his promise to me, joined the Army after promising he never would, and off they went, the brave Landry men to fight in Vietnam. Off they went in their damn uniforms. And there I stood, a child, waving good-bye and crying." She dashed the tears from her face. "I will never go through that again. Excuse me, Colonel Hampton, but I must check with Jane and Fred and make sure all our guests have returned safely. I'll call you when supper is ready." She left the room, calling, "Come, Samson."

Samson wagged his tail as he watched her go, but he didn't budge from his comfortable spot on the floor.

"That was a direct order, soldier," Mark said to the dog. "You can't disobey your commanding officer." Samson just wagged his tail faster. Mark leaned back against the desk and picked up the glass cube. "It's lonely in there, right, butterfly? I'd bet on it. Come on, Eden. Let me in."

He carefully set down the cube and shook his head. If he didn't quit talking to dogs and butterflies trapped in crystal, he'd be taken away to a padded room.

Mark left the library and built a fire in the living room. Samson stayed at his elbow, supervising every move and slowing down the whole operation. At last, when the fire was blazing away, Mark settled on the sofa, and Samson sprawled across his feet.

"You weigh a ton," he said, peering at the dog. "Could we discuss this, buddy? I need those feet."

He heard the telephone ring. A minute later Eden appeared in the doorway.

"Mark, the phone is for you."

"I'll take it in the library. Call your dog, will you? I'm being held captive here."

"Samson, come." Samson didn't move. "Samson, peanut butter." The dog was up and running, and Eden shrugged. "What can I say? He's crazy about peanut butter."

Mark laughed as he strode into the library. He snatched up the phone. "Hampton."

"General Meyers. Johnson has been living with a woman for the past year or so. She's in a secretarial pool for senators on the hill. Her last name is Becker."

"Why do I get the feeling I don't want to hear her first name?" Mark asked, rubbing his forehead.

"You don't. Her name is Anna. She left work mid-morning on Friday, saying she didn't feel well. She hasn't been seen since. Mark, Anna Becker is missing."

Mark's jaw tightened, and he said the only thing that seemed to fit what he'd just been told.

"Hell."

Four

Mark awoke at dawn the next morning to the sound of a howling wind and snow whipping against the window.

Wonderful, he thought with disgust, pressing the heels of his hands to his eyes. From what he could hear, and would no doubt see when he investigated the situation, there would be no search parties looking for Bill Johnson that day.

He threw back the blankets and swung his feet to the floor. Which would also mean, he realized, that he would spend the day with Eden. Interesting thought. He'd hardly seen her the night before. After dinner she'd headed for the library, explaining that she had paperwork to catch up on. After several hours, as Mark sat by the fire reading a book, she'd emerged and announced she was going to bed. And that had been that.

Well, not today, Mark decided firmly. Today he

was sticking to her like glue, and he had every intention of finding out a great deal more about the elusive Miss Landry.

Many hours later, Mark lay in bed, his hands laced under his head, staring up into the darkness. He had pleaded further jet lag and bid Eden good night shortly after ten o'clock. Now, at one A.M., he was still wide awake, and his muscles were beginning to twitch from tension.

What he had actually done, he admitted dryly, was hightail it to his room at the first opportunity to get away from Eden. She was driving him right out of his mind. His libido had gone into overdrive as the day progressed, his blood flowing heavy and hot each time she came near him.

He'd thought of a hundred things he wanted to ask her about herself. He wanted to know all there was to know, from who had been her best friend in first grade to why she was running a ranch in Montana.

Instead they'd chatted off and on about the weather, the selection of books in the library, whether she watched sports events on the wide-screen television. He had been delighted when she said that she was an avid football fan. And when she'd wrinkled her nose in disgust at his praising of the Washington Redskins, they'd cheerfully argued the merits of the various teams.

They'd watched an old movie on television, sharing a huge bowl of buttered popcorn, then later Mark had helped prepare a simple dinner of soup and grilled cheese sandwiches. John Chambers had called to say the weather was clearing and that they would go out the next day to search for Bill.

Yet beneath the surface of that relaxed, comfortable, sharing day had been a current of tension, a crackle of awareness and heightened senses. Mark knew it had been due in part to Bill Johnson, and now Anna Becker, being missing. After dinner he had told Eden of General Meyers's news and she had gasped, her eyes widening in shock.

"What does all this mean?" she'd asked him.

"I'm trying to piece it together. Look, I'm going to trust you, okay? But what I'm about to tell you goes no further than this room."

"Of course."

He told her a little bit of what was going on, simply alluding to the existence of Bill Johnson's walking around with top-secret information. He did explain the sudden disappearance of Anna Becker, and that the finding of the unicorns indicated something much more complicated than a man lost in the woods was going on.

"It's frightening," she said. "Are you with Intelligence?"

"I was for many years. Fieldwork, both as a pilot and on the ground. Now I have a desk job in Washington doing security clearances for personnel involved in various levels of classified work."

"I see. So, they're calling on your expertise from the past to solve this thing."

He shrugged. "Something like that. Anyway, that's where we stand now. I'll fill Chambers in on a need-to-know basis." He paused. "Let's give it a rest for tonight and talk about something else."

Mark shifted on the bed, trying once again to find

a comfortable position that would lull him to sleep. He had learned a few details about Eden, but more, he'd been disturbed by that nearly palpable tension between them. The sexual electricity could have lit a fire without a match.

Eden, he knew, was not immune to what was taking place. She'd become increasingly jumpy as the evening progressed, flipping through magazines, continually rising to poke at the burning logs, avoiding looking directly at him. When she'd suggested they have a brandy, she'd nearly thrown the snifter into his hand rather than risk having their fingers touch.

He had finally had enough, mumbled his bit about jet lag and escaped to his room. And now, there he was, wide awake, his body one tight coil, his mind a jumble.

"Damn," he said, punching his pillow. He was acting like a horny teenager. He ached with the need to pull Eden into his arms, to kiss her, and hold her, then to carry her to bed and make sweet, slow love to her through the night.

Oh, Lord, he thought, shaking his head. Why Eden? Why, after all the women he'd known through the years, was Eden Landry knocking him for a loop? Why did he feel driven to bring the sparkle of joy back to her green eyes? What was this woman doing to his control, to his total command of his mind and body? Dammit, she was driving him nuts!

With a groan, he rolled onto his stomach, gave his pillow another solid punch, then forced himself to relax. At last the fatiguing tension of the long day caught up with him, and he slept, tossing and turning through the remaining hours in the night.

• • •

Mark awoke to the sensation of something cold and wet pressing against his cheek. He opened one eye to find himself looking at Samson, who stood by the bed, his tail wagging cheerfully. Samson, Mark was foggily convinced, was smiling.

"How's life?" he mumbled. The wagging tail increased its tempo and the dog sloppily licked Mark's beard-roughened cheek. "Knock it off, dog. You're not my idea of great stuff to wake up to, thank you very much."

Mark lifted his head to see that the bedroom door stood open. He had apparently not shut it tight the night before, and Samson had simply leaned his bulky body against it and entered. He glanced at the clock, knew he had to get up in order to be ready to meet John Chambers, then looked at the open door again.

Darn it, where was Eden? he wondered. He had to get all the way across the room to the bathroom, and he didn't have a stitch on.

"Eden," he said to Samson. The dog sat down. "Oh, really? What happens if I say 'sit'?" Samson thumped his tail on the floor. "Oh, for Pete's sake." Mark pushed the pillow behind him and sat up against the headboard, the blankets pulled to his waist. "Get out of the way, Samson, so I can make a run for it." Samson laid down. "Cripes."

"Samson, where are you?" Eden whispered from the hallway. "Samson?"

"He's in here," Mark called.

She appeared in the open doorway. "Samson, what are you—" She stopped speaking as her gaze fell on Mark.

Dear heaven, she thought. She'd assumed Mark was up and dressed. But he most certainly wasn't.

She should have known he'd have a beautiful chest. It stood to reason it would be broad and solid, covered in swirling dark hair that disappeared in a narrowing line beneath the blankets.

What she hadn't anticipated was what the sight of that chest, and his tousled hair, and the dark stubble of beard on his handsome face would do to her heart rate. A half-naked Mark Hampton just waking up in the morning was a flustering sight to behold.

"Good morning," he said, smiling at her.

That capped it, she thought, feeling heat curl deep inside her. The smile really did it. The man didn't play fair. But then, she recalled, he'd said as much. He'd admitted he didn't always fight fair when he was after something he really wanted.

"Yes, good morning," she said, amazed that her voice was working. "I was just looking for Samson."

"Well, he's blocking my path from here to the shower," Mark said pleasantly. "I could go over him, I suppose, but I also have the problem of not being into streaking in front of my hostess. Unless, of course, it wouldn't bother you. Just say the word and I'll sprint right across the room."

Go for it, Hampton, she thought dreamily, then she blinked. "Oh!"

"Well?" he asked, all innocence as he gripped the top of the blankets with one hand. "What shall it be? You're calling the shots here, Miss Landry."

She pointed a finger at him. "Don't you move, Colonel! Samson, come." The dog beat his tail wildly on the floor. "Dammit, Samson, peanut butter!" Samson lunged to his feet and barreled across the room, nearly knocking Eden over as he bounded out the door.

"Remarkable dog," Mark said. "He's trained in code. It really is amazing. You've done quite a job with that animal, Eden."

She glared at him, then shut the door closed behind her with a resounding thud. The sound of Mark's rich laughter followed her as she strode down the hall.

Arrogant and rude, she fumed, as she entered the kitchen. Mark Hampton was rude and arrogant. And magnificent. She'd gawked at him like a blushing teenager. The only saving grace was that the smug colonel had no idea how she'd tossed and turned through the night, imagining him coming to her, taking her into his arms and . . .

"Stop it, Eden," she muttered, reaching for a frying pan. Never before had she fantasized in such explicit detail about a man making love to her as she'd done last night. When she'd finally slept, she'd even *dreamed* of becoming one with Mark in a glorious union. She'd awakened to find her heart racing and heat pouring through her entire body. How disgusting! How juvenile! What on earth was the matter with her?

Samson whined, bringing Eden from her thoughts, and she plopped a spoonful of the promised peanut butter into his dish. As she scrambled the eggs, she thought about the strange tension between her and Mark the previous day.

He had seemed to fill her large house to overflowing, his vibrant masculinity reaching out to her, touching her wherever she was with him. Her usual peace as she'd attended to business and relaxed had been shattered by a potent awareness of him, leaving her tense and edgy and unable to sleep.

Okay, she thought. Truth time. Yes, she was very attracted to Mark Hampton. And, yes, their kisses had been more overpowering, more enjoyable than any she'd ever experienced before. And yes, darn it, she wanted to make love with him. But it wasn't going to happen.

She shook her head as she poured the frothy eggs into the frying pan. No, she wasn't going to succumb to Mark's pull on her senses or to her simmering desire for him. She couldn't, because she would be left behind to cry once again as she watched a uniformed man walk away from her, leaving her alone and lonely.

"Something smells good," Mark said as he strode into the kitchen. "Peanut butter for one. I smell coffee too."

"Help yourself," she said, not looking at him. "The eggs and toast will be ready in a minute." She slid a sideways glance at him, saw his snug jeans and black flannel shirt, and redirected her attention to the frying pan.

"Anything I can do to help?" he asked.

Leave! Go away! she wanted to yell. "No."

He poured himself a mug of coffee and sat down at the table. "Have you heard a weather report?"

"Yes." She scooped the eggs onto a platter. "John was right. The snowstorm stopped in the night, but the drifts are high. I'm not sure how far we'll get on the horses. There's a threat of another storm moving in."

"I wish you'd reconsider about going," he said quietly. "There could very well be more than snow to worry about out there. I'd feel better knowing you were here, safe from harm."

"No, I'm going," she said, placing the platter on the table. "I was miserable here the day before yesterday, wondering what was going on. I'd rather be out there seeing for myself."

"Are you forgetting that someone took a shot at one of John's deputies?"

"A hunter."

"We don't know that for sure. It could have been a warning of some kind."

"Or maybe it wasn't." She brought a plate of toast and her coffee mug to the table and sat down opposite him. "I'm going with you, Mark."

He frowned. "You're stubborn."

She took a sip of coffee. "Yes, I suppose I am at times. Use your energy to eat your breakfast instead of trying to talk me out of going along. We have a hard day ahead of us. You'll need a hat and an extra sweater. There's a Stetson here you can use."

"Fine," he said gruffly.

"Frustrating, isn't it?' she said cheerfully. "You'd love to give me an order to stay put, then have me say 'Yes, sir,' and that would be that. Welcome to the world of civilians, Colonel. We have minds of our own."

"Cute," he said, heaping eggs onto his plate.

They ate in silence for several minutes, then Eden got up and refilled their coffee mugs. Mark watched her move across the kitchen, enjoying the way her corduroys fit. When she sat down again he noticed how her bulky green sweater matched her eyes.

"I guess the sheriff will be here soon," he said.

"Yes."

"He's a nice guy. Knows his stuff."

She took a bite of toast and nodded.

"He didn't seem terribly upset that I was staying here with you. Of course, maybe he didn't realize I was actually sleeping in the house."

Eden picked up her mug, then sat it back down. "Just what is it you want to know, Mark?" she asked. "For an Intelligence officer, you're certainly a fumble-mouth this morning. I thought you guys were experts at wiggling information out of people without having them realize you were doing it."

Scowling, Mark jabbed his fork into his eggs. "All right, Miss Know-it-all, we'll do this up-front. Are you and John Chambers lovers?"

She stiffened in her chair. "What? How dare you ask me such a question."

"Hey," he said, raising his hands in a gesture of peace, "I'm just gathering my facts, and you said yourself my usual smooth Intelligence manner was under par today. So? What's with you and Chambers?"

"That is none of your business," she said, hiding behind her mug.

He looked directly into her eyes, and his voice was low when he spoke. "Isn't it, Eden? There's something happening between us that is beyond mere physical attraction."

"No," she whispered. "No, there isn't."

He caught her free hand in his. "Yes, there is. You felt it just as I did when I kissed you. And we both felt it in this house all day yesterday. It's here now." He stroked the top of her hand with his thumb. "Feel the heat of our hands, Eden? It's electric, charged. Is it traveling through you like it is through me?"

"No," she said, attempting to pull her hand free. He tightened his hold. "Stop it."

"No, I won't," he said, leaning toward her. "I'm not afraid to find out what is happening between us, but you obviously are. You're all tucked away behind your protective walls, just like the butterfly in the glass cube. I still believe that it's lonely in there, behind those walls. Isn't it lonely?"

"Yes. No. Leave me alone, Mark."

"Is John Chambers in the picture?"

"No. We're friends, just friends. We go to a movie sometimes, or out to dinner, but— Darn you, why am I telling you this?"

"Because I asked, because I need to know what I'm up against." He smiled. "It appears that my only competition is those walls of yours. Fair enough. Oh, and . . . Eden, please don't waste your breath on a spiel about me seeing you only as a challenge, a game of sorts, while I'm out here in the middle of nowhere. I'm not playing around. I intend to know exactly what this is between us."

She yanked her hand free. "Have a good time," she said tightly, "because I'm not the least bit interested in knowing."

He chuckled and drained his coffee mug.

"What is that supposed to mean?" she asked, smacking the table with her hand.

"What is what supposed to mean?" His expression was all innocence.

"That— that sexy little chuckle, that smug, male . . . noise. Oh, forget it. You're driving me crazy." She folded her arms across her chest.

"Lady, that is my point. You're driving me crazy too." He paused. "Did you sleep well last night, Eden?"

"What?"

"Or did you toss and turn like I did, fantasizing about having you in my arms, in my bed, making love to you? We're going to be sensational together. You know that, don't you? Slow, sweet lovemaking, Eden. Hours and hours of slow, sweet lovemaking."

His voice floated over her, touching her, caressing, his words creating a hazy mist as she envisioned everything that he was saying. Vivid fantasies from last night flitted before her eyes, and heat flared deep within her, moving throughout her with insistent fingers.

Dear heaven, how she wanted this man, yearned to bring to reality all that she had imagined. Yes, she knew their joining would be glorious. He would fill her body with all that he was and fill the empty, lonely chambers of her heart and soul as well.

"Don't be afraid of me," he said. "I won't hurt you, I swear it. Please, Eden, give us a chance."

"I can't," she said, her voice trembling. "I don't want . . ."

"Eden, please, listen to me."

"No, no," she said, shaking her head.

He got up and walked around the table. Gripping her shoulders, he pulled her gently from her chair, then wrapped his arms around her, holding her close to his body.

She buried her face against his chest as she circled his waist with her arms. She was past asking herself why she was allowing him to hold her this way, knowing only that she wanted to be there in the strong, safe haven of his embrace.

How was it possible, she wondered, that with Mark she had the sense of coming home? How was it possible that the serene, peaceful existence she'd created for herself on the Lazy L now seemed lonely when she envisioned herself there without Mark? And how was it possible that she knew, deep within the very heart of herself, that if she made love with Mark Hampton it would be so very *right*?

Mark felt her relax, felt the tension ebb from her. He breathed in the aroma of her perfume as his body reacted to the feel of her womanly curves pressed against him. She was filling him, though he hadn't known he was empty. With Eden in his arms, he felt a sense of completeness, of knowing who he was as a total man.

What did all of this mean? he wondered. His passion for her was like none before, but there was so much more churning in his mind and his heart. The emotions were new and unfamiliar, but he welcomed them, rejoiced in them. The need to protect her, and also to make her smile, the desire to laugh and share with her, and to plan for the tomorrows, were all there, warming him, filing him to overflowing. What was this? Unless . . .

"Eden," he said huskily, "I think . . . I think I'm falling in love with you."

She stiffened, then slowly tilted her head back to look up at him, her eyes wide with shock.

"I beg your pardon?" she asked, her voice not quite steady.

He didn't release her. "Yes," he said, smiling down at her, "I really think that's what might be happening here. I can remember my father telling me that when love happened I might as well give up and give in, because there was no escaping it. He also said I'd be a foolish man if I didn't recognize it and rejoice in it when it came into my life."

"But . . ."

"I haven't been running from love," he went on, needing to explain. "Granted, I haven't been looking either. I've just sort of been going through life waiting to see if my number would be drawn. And now, here you are."

"Oh, no." She started to pull back from him.

"I feel like I've been run over by a truck," he said, and his smile broadened. "But, it's sensational, really great. Oh, yes, Eden, this is love, all right. I've got it all squared away now. Eden Landry, I, Mark Hampton, am falling in love with you."

She wiggled out of his arms. "You are not," she said firmly.

"Oh, but I am," he said, extremely pleased with himself.

"Would you stop it? I don't want to hear any more of your nonsense. It's a unique seduction routine, but I'm not falling for it. Just put a cork in it, Colonel."

He frowned and ran his hand over his chin. "You don't believe me. Damn." He smiled again. "Well, no problem. I'll just convince you that I'm telling the truth, that's all. I've never fallen in love before. Now that I've found you, Eden"—his smile faded—"I'm sure as hell not going to lose you."

She backed up until she bumped against the table. "I don't want to hear this."

He followed her, moving close enough to weave his fingers through the waves of her silken hair.

"Don't be frightened," he said softly. "Don't be afraid of me, or of yourself. Everything is going to work out just fine, you'll see." He lowered his head toward hers. "Please don't be frightened, Eden."

Frightened? she thought wildly. She was scared to death! This man was a lunatic, a bona fide nut case. He was—

Her thoughts skidded to a halt as Mark's mouth melted over hers. A wimper of protest caught in her throat, and then she was lost as she returned the kiss in total abandon. Shimmering heat consumed her as desire pulsed deep within her.

Mark was falling in love with her? she wondered dreamily. Was that what had been happening to her too? Was she falling in love with Mark Hampton? No! No!

She pushed against his chest. "No!"

Mark gazed down at her, his gray eyes smoky with desire. "Huh? What?"

"You can't love me," she said shaking her head.

He drew a steadying breath. "Well, too late. I already do."

She narrowed her eyes and stared at him. He met her gaze. "Oh, dear heaven," she whispered, "you do. I can see in your eyes."

"I wouldn't lie about something this important, Eden. I don't know how or why it happened so fast. Maybe . . ."

He paused and considered these last two days with Eden, and his last several months in Washington.

"Maybe," he continued thoughtfully, "I've subconsciously been looking for a woman like you for a long time. Just by being yourself, you've touched a need deep inside me, filled an emptiness in me that I didn't realize was there." He smiled at her. "And I know you feel something special for me, Eden, but you probably need time to sort it through. I'll try to be patient until you realize that you love me, and that you don't need those walls of yours anymore."

An almost hysterical giggle escaped from her lips. "I don't believe this. I was doing fine, my life was in order, and now here you are, turning things upside down and backward."

He shrugged. "Love is like that sometimes, I guess."

"*You* are in love," she said, poking him in the chest. "*I* am not." Or was she? Oh, Lord, she really couldn't handle this. She refused to be in love with this blue-suiter, this colonel, this fly-boy, this man.

So what if he evoked such overwhelming desire within her? So what if the thought of being at the Lazy L without him caused tears to burn her eyes? So what if the mere sight of him brought a flush to her cheeks and a rerun of her wanton fantasies? It didn't mean a thing . . . except that she might be falling in love with Colonel Mark Hampton, of the United States Air Force.

He brushed his thumb over her lips. "Give it some time. You'll figure it all out."

She lifted her chin. "You're awful sure of yourself. And arrogant. You're arrogant, Mark."

"Me? I'm not arrogant. I'm a man in love. A man whose entire future hinges on your not running farther behind those walls of yours. There is nothing standing in our way that we can't solve together. But, Eden, you have to face your feelings and be wiling to admit them. We'll take one step at a time here. Slow and easy."

"Slow and easy?" She waved a hand in the air. "You call this slow and easy? You swooshed in here like a tornado and now you're upsetting everything in your path, including me."

"Oh." He frowned. "Well, from now on we'll take it slow and easy. Don't worry about a thing."

She pressed her hands to her temples. "I really can't believe this. Things like this don't happen to normal people."

He grinned. "Sure they do. People fall in love every day of the week. Even on crummy Mondays."

There was a knock at the front door.

"That's John," she said. "Oh, thank God, a sane human being is at the door." She hurried out of the kitchen.

Mark chuckled and followed slowly behind. He was in love with Eden, he thought. It was great. After all these years, love had finally called his name. He couldn't lose her now. He had a rough battle ahead of him, he knew that, but he intended to win. Eden would come to realize that she loved him. She had to, or he'd end up with a shattered heart. Eden Landry was going to be his!

When Mark entered the living room, John Chambers was rubbing his hands together in front of the fire.

"Hello, John," he said.

John nodded at him. "Mark. It's cold out there this morning. Listen, I don't know how far we're going to get today. The snowdrifts are high, and the horses are going to have trouble getting through. They'll tire quickly too. This could be a wasted effort, but we'll give it our best shot."

"Fair enough," Mark said.

"I was thinking," John went on, "that we should ask the National Guard to fly a helicopter over the area. They won't be able to check the ground much, because the trees are so thick, but if Bill Johnson is holed up in a cabin, they'd see smoke from a chimney. I assume he'd have enough sense to start a fire and keep warm."

"Good idea," Mark said, "but let me make a call to get a chopper out here. I don't want to involve the National Guard in this."

John shrugged. "Fine."

"I won't be long," Mark said, heading toward the library. "Then we'll hit the road."

As Mark left the room, John turned from the fire. "You're awfully quiet this morning, Eden."

"What? Oh, I'm fine, just . . . quiet."

"It's going to be rough out there. Why don't you stay here?"

"No." She stared at the closed library door.

John followed her gaze, then looked at her again. "There's something going on between you and Mark, isn't there?"

She snapped her head around. "Me and Mark? Don't be silly. I hardly know the man. Besides, he's in the military. You know how I feel about that. That in itself is enough to . . . Besides, he's not my type. He's arrogant, even rude at times. I really don't . . . Why are you standing there with an enormous grin on your face, John Chambers?"

He laughed. "Because you're babbling and you're flustered. Your cheeks are bright pink. I'm witnessing Eden Landry coming unglued, something I've never seen before."

"Oh, hush," she said. She crossed her arms and stared at the floor. "Just hush."

John became serious. "You know, Eden, when

you first came here I'd hoped you and I . . . Well, it just wasn't meant to be, and I've cherished our friendship. Because we're friends, because you're important to me, I'm going to say this. Don't run, Eden, not anymore. If you're feeling something special for Mark, don't run from it."

She slowly lifted her head. "I'm frightened, John. It's all happening so quickly, and I can't sort it out."

"Take the time you need. But be fair. Remember that Mark isn't a uniform, he's a man. Judge the man, not the clothes, not the career."

"I don't know if I can do that."

"If you love him, you will."

"How will I know if I'm in love with him?"

"Believe me, Eden," he said quietly, turning back to gaze into the fire, "you'll know."

In the library, Mark sat in the leather chair behind the desk.

"Good," he said into the phone. "I don't know when we'll be back today, but I'll call in as soon as I can to see if the helicopter pilot spotted anything."

"Fine," General Meyers said.

"Keep that entire Project Unicorn team under tight security, General. Nobody moves an inch without an escort."

"Any theories yet, Mark?"

"Not really. I suspect that are a lot of pieces to this puzzle. Maybe something will click when I get out there and see where Bill was headed. I'm just not sure how far we can get because of the snow."

"We've got to clear this mess up as quickly as possible."

"I know, but nobody told Mother Nature that. I'll call you later, sir."

"All right, Mark."

"Have a nice day, General."

"You're not a funny man, Colonel. Good-bye."

Mark replaced the receiver and stood. As he started across the room, he hesitated, stopping to gaze at the sofa and fireplace, remembering the scenario he'd painted in his mind of being with his children and his wife, Eden.

He couldn't lose her, he thought yet again. He couldn't lose his Eden.

Five

When Mark came out of the library, he sensed a tension in the air as both Eden and John looked at him. They'd been talking about him, he thought. He'd make a book on it. And he'd give a month's pay to know what had been said. Unfortunately, mind reading had not been part of his training for Intelligence assignments.

"All set," he said. "An Air Force helicopter will be in the area as soon as possible, and the pilot's report will be called in to me later. I'll keep you posted on what he says, John."

"Sounds good." John crossed the room and pulled two maps out of his jacket pocket. "Let's take a look at these."

In the kitchen he spread both maps out on the table. One was marked with black lines, circles, and checks. He took a pen from his pocket and reached for the unmarked map.

"Okay, Mark, this is where I found the unicorn," he said, making a circle on the paper. "And here is where Pete was shot at. You can see it was less than a quarter of a mile away. There are three cabins in that area . . . here . . . here . . . and here. I looked in each one, but there was no sign of anyone."

"Got it," Mark said, nodding.

John went on. "We also covered this whole area to the right of that and found nothing. Today I plan to go farther to the right . . . here . . . then up over the top of the ridge, providing we can get that far in the snow."

"All right," Mark said. "You go ahead with your plans. I'm going back to the first section where the unicorn was found, then I'll work my way straight up. I realize you covered that area, John, but I need to backtrack it because of the unicorn. If I can get through the drifts, I'll go higher than you did, hopefully make it to the top and over the ridge."

"What if the helicopter spots something?" Eden asked. "You won't have any way of knowing."

"I realize that," Mark said. "It's not a great plan, but I don't want to sit around waiting for communication equipment to be brought or dropped in. We'll do our part on the ground, the pilot will do his thing in the air, and we'll compare notes later. That's the best we can do for today." He picked up the freshly marked map. "Okay, let's hit the road."

There was a knock at the kitchen door, and Eden went to answer it.

"Oh, good morning, Jane," she said. "Come in."

A short woman, appearing to be in her fifties, entered the kitchen. She had gray hair, wore no makeup, and was bundled up in an oversized, heavy black coat.

"Sorry to be pounding at your door so early," she said. "I just thought you should know that all the hunters are leaving the Lazy L. They decided not to try to make their way through the snowdrifts. I'll straighten and clean the cabins once they're gone. I told them you'd be speaking to them about refunds for cutting their stays short."

"Well, at least we won't have more lost souls out there," Eden said. "I'm leaving with the search team now, Jane. Could you tell the hunters I'll be in touch by mail as quickly as possible? Don't tell them we're looking for a lost man, just say I'm tied up at the moment."

"Sure thing," Jane said. "Hello, John," she added.

"Hello, Jane. How's Fred?"

"Fit as a fiddle." She looked at Mark.

"This is Mark Hampton," Eden said. "He's helping with the search."

Jane frowned. "You're not from around here."

"No, ma'am," Mark said. "I'm an old friend of John's. I'm just helping out my buddy here. I take it you've lived in this area a long time."

"Thirty years. Me and Fred been working on this ranch since Henry Foster bought this land and put up the buildings. It was a working ranch back in those days, cattle, horses, cowboys to feed. Those were good times. Now we just cater to rich city fellas who kill animals for the joy of it. Hunting should be done for food, not for the pleasure of killing for a trophy to hang on a wall."

Eden smiled. "Thank you for coming to tell me the

hunters are leaving. I don't know when I'll be back. Could you take Samson with you?"

Jane's stern features immediately softened. "Oh, sure, I'll take care of that big baby. Where is he? Samson! Come!"

Samson bounded into the kitchen, nearly falling over his feet.

Eden rolled her eyes heavenward. "He obeys everyone but me." She scratched the dog behind the ears. "Be a good boy for Jane, Samson."

"He always is," Jane said, then went out the back door with Samson trotting happily at her side.

"She sure doesn't like hunters," Mark said. "Aren't you afraid she'll insult your guests, Eden?"

"We reached an agreement five years ago when I bought this place. The Sawyers wanted to stay, and I made it clear that their opinions had to be kept to themselves. In the summer we get families and run more of a dude ranch. It's only in the winter, when it's all hunters, that the Sawyers get uptight. They never say anything to the guests, though."

"You bought this place from that Henry Foster?" Mark asked.

"No, he had died. There was no immediate family or will, so it was an estate sale. I had the cabins built and brought in some gentle horses for less-experienced riders. The Sawyers were already living in that larger cabin."

"For thirty years?" Mark asked.

"Yes. Fred brought Jane here as his bride, and they've been here ever since."

"Do they have children?"

"A daughter. Jane mentioned her only once, then changed the subject very quickly. She's never visited her parents since I've been here. I get the impression that there are hard feelings between them."

"I sure didn't know they had a daughter," John said, "and I grew up around here. She must have gone to school in town."

"Humor me, John," Mark said, "and check that out very quietly when we get back today, will you?"

John nodded. "I'm curious myself. I'll let you know what I find out. Ready to go?"

"Let's do it," Mark said. "Eden, I don't suppose you'd change your mind about—"

"No."

Mark frowned, John laughed, and the three left the kitchen.

The air was biting cold, the sky was a bright blue, and the snow looked like shimmering diamonds in all directions. John drove the Bronco with the skill of a man accustomed to handling a heavy vehicle on rough terrain. They left the Lazy L and traveled for several miles on the rutted dirt road before turning onto a narrower dirt stretch that headed steadily upward. No one spoke, each lost in thought.

"There are dark clouds against the horizon," Eden said finally, breaking the silence. "The weather report this morning said to expect more snow."

"Keep an eye on those clouds," John said. "Head back before . . . Well, I guess I don't have to tell you all this, Mark. You're trained in this stuff."

"Do you have walkie-talkies?" Mark asked.

John snorted in disgust. "No. I go before the town council every year at budget time asking for better equipment. They're just good old boys who believe a gun fired in the air is the best kind of communication in the wilds. We don't need, as they say, 'those highfalutin', big-city toys.' It's no wonder the Sawyers's daughter didn't want to stay around here. It's like living back in the dark ages."

Eden looked at John. "I thought you said you didn't know until today that they had a daughter."

He glanced at her, then back at the road. "Oh, well, I didn't. I'm just guessing that she took off as quickly as she could for the real world, that's all."

"But I've always felt that you loved it here, John," Eden said. "You grew up here and came home as soon as you graduated from college."

"It's okay here," he said quickly. "There are the guys and horses up ahead."

Mark narrowed his eyes as he studied John, then rubbed his hand thoughtfully over his chin. He glanced at Eden, but she was still looking at John.

Interesting, Mark thought. Very interesting. There was more to Sheriff John Chambers than met the eye. There had been a bitter edge to his voice for a while there. Very, very interesting.

The three deputies waiting by the trucks and horse trailers were introduced to Mark as Pete, Jimmy Joe, and Jasper. Because Mark was wearing his heavy Air Force jacket, John simply said that Mark was a guest at the Lazy L and had volunteered to help, since he'd been trained in search and rescue. The deputies shrugged, nodded, and shook Mark's hand.

John spread his map out on the hood of one of the trucks. "We'll go up over here," he said, pointing to an area on the map. "Mark is going back into the first section."

"How come?" Pete asked. "We covered that going and coming. I got shot at coming, remember?"

"He's checking it again," John said tightly. "Okay with you, Pete?"

"Yeah, sure, John. I didn't mean nothing. Just wondered why he was . . . Never mind."

"If the drifts are too high, come back here," John said. "Otherwise, keep at it. We'll call it quits by three. Everyone be here at the trucks at three sharp, so allow time to work your way down. The storm brewing over there is due about five. I want plenty of leeway. If the storm moves in early, hightail it back here. Jasper, did you take care of the saddlebags?"

"Yep. There's thermoses of coffee, sandwiches, some jerky, and—"

"Yeah, okay, let's go," John interrupted.

"I'll go with Mark," Eden said.

"Why?" John asked. "He's better trained than these guys. He's not about to get lost, Eden."

"I know where the abandoned cabins are," she said. "I know you marked them on his map, but it will be much easier for us to recheck them because I know exactly where they are. With this much snow on the ground, those maps are hard to follow, John. You know that."

He nodded, then refolded his map without speaking and put it in his pocket.

Eden looked questioningly at John, then glanced up at Mark, who was watching the sheriff intently.

Something was wrong here, she thought worriedly. John was acting so strangely, like someone she didn't know. Maybe she was imagining it, but . . .

"Let's go," Mark said quietly to her.

"Yes, all right." She flipped the fur-lined hood to her jacket up over her head and pulled on her gloves.

Mark put on his gloves, too, then tugged the Stetson Eden had loaned him firmly forward on his head.

Wonderful, she thought dryly. Now Mark looked like the Marlboro man, with less age on his face, though. Devastatingly handsome and rugged. He really wasn't kidding when he said he didn't always fight fair. He was just so darn male.

John pointed to their horses, and Mark swung into the saddle with a lazy, graceful motion that caused a shiver to dance along Eden's spine. She mounted her horse, and smiled at the three deputies.

"Good luck," she said. "Let's hope we find Bill today. See you later, John."

"Yeah," he said. "Be careful. Be very careful up there."

"Yes, of course, we will."

John and the deputies turned their horses and set out.

Eden looked at Mark. "Ready to go?"

He pulled his gaze from the four figures moving off in the other direction. "Sure."

They started upward, the surefooted horses carrying them slowly forward. Ten minutes passed.

"I can't stand it," she said. "If I don't say something, I'll pop a seam."

"Hmm?" He glanced over at her.

"It's John. I don't know, Mark, there was something different about him after we left the house."

"Yep."

"That's all you have to say?" she asked, frowning at him.

"Well, I don't know him that well, but there was definitely a change in personality. He wasn't the laid-back Mister Nice Guy I'd seen up until now."

"I tried to tell myself I was imagining it."

"No, you weren't. Don't worry about it." He'd worry enough for both of them. "This is beautiful country. Cold as hell, but picture perfect. Those hills and trees covered with snow look like a painting." And his damn knee was already starting to ache from the damp cold. It was going to be a very long day. "Really pretty."

"Yes, it is," she said. "But the drifts are getting deeper. This is shaping up to be slow going, and the horses will get exhausted quickly."

"We'll go as far as we can. I have no intention of running these animals into the ground."

For the next hour, they didn't speak. They concentrated on staying in the saddle as the horses lunged their way upward through the increasingly deep snowdrifts.

"This is it," Eden said finally, gasping for breath. "This is the area where John found the unicorn. Oh, boy, I am ready for a break, and I'm sure this horse is too. There's flat land over there, Mark."

He nodded, and they urged the horses forward. Eden pulled on the reins and swung out of the saddle. She frowned as she watched Mark dismount slowly and cringe as his feet hit the ground.

"What's wrong?" she asked.

"Old war wound." He grinned. "That's what they always say in the movies."

"Is it true?" she asked quietly. "I saw the Purple Heart on your uniform. Were you wounded in Vietnam?"

He tied the reins to a tree limb. "Me? Naw. My plane was wounded. I just happened to be the guy flying it." He pulled a rolled tarp from behind the saddle. "Let's sit and take a breather. We need it as much as these horses. How about some coffee?"

"Yes, all right," she said, and opened her saddle-bag. She watched Mark covertly as he limped toward a tree. He brushed away the snow at the base and spread out the tarp. Clenching his jaw, he eased himself to the ground and massaged his right knee. "Hot coffee coming up," she said, forcing a lightness to her voice.

She settled next to him on the tarp and poured coffee into plastic mugs. He took a sip.

"Hits the spot," he said. "Thanks."

"Mark, what happened to your knee when your plane was . . . wounded?"

He stared into the steaming liquid in the mug. "It's old news. You don't want to hear—"

"Yes, I do. It happened to you, so that makes it important."

He met her gaze. "Does it?" he asked, his voice low and serious.

"Yes," she whispered.

"It works both ways, you know, the sharing. Remember that the next time I ask you something about yourself. I love you, Eden. There's no room in our lives for secrets. Everything has to be up-front, no matter how painful it might be. There can't be ghosts hovering around, keeping us apart. I know you haven't said you love me, but you'll never be able to find out whether you do if you're all cluttered up inside with the past. You've built those walls of yours out of memories, and they have to be torn down."

"I . . . I'm very confused, Mark. Things have happened so quickly between us."

"I know." He took a deep breath and let it out slowly. "So, we start somewhere, with something, I guess. My wounded plane is as good a place as any. It's *my* painful ghost, Eden, and I'm willing to lay it all out for you."

"No. I have no right to ask you to relive something that's a nightmare for you."

"Yes, you do, because I love you. I shouldn't keep it inside, taking up space that could be filled with you."

"But, Mark—"

"I flew fighter jets in Vietnam," he said. He swallowed more coffee and his gaze settled on a spot somewhere in the distance. His voice was low and flat when he spoke again. "I did three tours of duty in that hellhole. I was ground cover for the troops so the helicopters could get in to pick them up. It was low, tight flying, and I had to make sure my spray of bullets didn't hit our own men."

"Dear heaven," she whispered.

"It wasn't a thrill a minute, I'll tell you that. Anyway, I was just about due to ship home, only had a couple of weeks to go. We got a coded signal that some guys were trapped in the jungle and the enemy was closing in."

"And you went."

"Yes. I took off in the jet and flew cover for a trooper chopper. It was dusk, really hard to see. We were picking up the men's signal, but knew the enemy was equipped to hear it too. I flew low, sprayed the area with gunfire, the chopper landed, and our boys came barreling out of the jungle. I circled and circled until the helicopter lifted off the ground. I stayed behind and riddled the area with bullets to give the chopper a good head start."

"And?" she asked, looking at him anxiously.

He didn't speak, his eyes still focused on the unknown spot in the distance. A shadow of pain flickered across his face.

Oh, Lord, she thought, blinking away her tears. He was back in Vietnam, reliving it all. She could see the horror of it in his eyes. It was costing him so much to do this, and he was doing it for her.

He shook his head and blinked, as though coming out of a trance. He drained his coffee mug, then reached for her hand. He rested it on his thigh and stared down at their entwined fingers.

"My plane was hit by ground fire as I left the area," he said hoarsely. "I was losing fuel. I flew low, just above the trees, talking to that plane like it was a human being. I knew I was going to go down in the jungle, and I kept saying to the plane, 'Keep your wings on, honey.' Dumb, huh? You can't fly a plane without fuel, wings or not, but it was suddenly so damn important to me that those wings didn't shear off."

Unnoticed tears spilled onto Eden's cheeks.

" 'Keep your wings on, honey,' " he repeated. "I kept saying that, over and over. I went down . . . in the trees. The right wing came off like slicing a piece of pie. The plane flipped and my right knee was crushed."

"Oh, dear God."

His hold on her hand tightened. "I knew I had to get out of there to a clear area, or they'd never be able to pick me up. I crawled on my belly, dragging my leg. Crawling and crawling. So damn far. I had my signaling device, and it was a contest by then. Who would get to me first? Our guys, or theirs?" He drew a ragged breath. "They made it . . . they came for me . . . a fighter jet and a chopper . . . my buddies . . . they got me out."

"Oh, Mark," she said, a sob catching in her throat.

"The rest is history. They shipped me home, and I had four operations to rebuild my knee. I don't even limp, except when I'm in the cold and damp and it tightens up on me. I couldn't qualify to be an Air Force pilot anymore, though. They don't trust million-dollar aircraft to a guy with a trick knee. I can fly private planes, could even be an instructor as a civilian, but my blue-suiter, fly-boy days are over. That's it, Eden. My ghost. It was a long time ago. It was yesterday."

"Mark, it must have been so terrible, so painful."

He turned his head to look at her and saw the tears streaming down her face.

"Eden, no," he said, pulling her into his arms. "Don't cry. I didn't mean to make you cry. It happened, it's part of who I am, and you have a right to know about it. We don't ever have to talk about it again. No tears, Eden. I'm alive, which is a helluva lot to be thankful for."

"Yes. Yes, of course, it is," she said. She sniffled and lifted her head to look at him. "Thank you for telling me. I know it was very difficult for you to relive it all."

"I love you, Eden. There can't be any secrets, any ghosts, standing between us."

His mouth came down hard onto hers, his tongue plunging into her mouth. She felt a shudder rip through him, then the kiss gentled, as though he'd pushed away the last haunting pain. She clung to him, answering the demands of his lips and tongue, wanting to comfort him, to fill him with herself, only herself.

The cold and snow were forgotten as the heat of their rising passions consumed them. The flames licked throughout them as their kisses became feverish.

Mark slowly, reluctantly lifted his head, not wanting to end the promise of Eden's kiss, not wanting to leave the haven of her embrace. With her he was complete, and he knew her love would lay the ghosts and horror of the past to rest forever.

If only, he thought, she would look deep within herself to discover her love for him. He knew it was there, for the love he felt for her was too powerful and too right not to be reciprocated. First, though, he had to crush the walls surrounding her, without hurting the fragile butterfly within.

She opened her eyes, and they were dark with desire.

"Oh, Mark," she whispered.

He smiled gently at her. "I know." He set her away from him. "This isn't exactly the time, or the place." A ragged breath escaped from his lips. "You are something, Miss Landry. If I dove into a snowdrift, do you think it would do the job of a cold shower?"

She laughed. "You'd probably only get a nice case of pneumonia for your trouble."

"True. Well, back to business. Where are those coffee mugs? They got lost in the shuffle."

She picked up the empty mugs they both had

dropped onto the tarp, then stood. Her legs were still trembling from their passionate kiss.

"How's your knee feeling?" she asked, looking down at him.

"Good as new." He got up in a smooth motion. "It'll be all right for a while anyway, then I'll have to rest it again. That's what you get for hanging out with an old man."

"A brave man," she said softly.

"No, Eden. What I did to survive in Nam weren't the actions of a hero. I wanted to live. I just couldn't accept the idea of dying without a fight, without doing everything I could to stay alive. Most men would have done the same thing under the circumstances."

"But not all men," she said, gazing off into the distance. "Some—some just give up. They see death as the best solution to the situation they find themselves in. They simply quit trying and . . ." Her voice trailed off.

Mark waited, watching her face, hoping she'd say more. Who was she talking about? he wondered. Her father? No, he didn't think so. He'd died of a heart attack. Her brother then? He'd died of wounds sustained in Vietnam years after the war had ended. What had happened to Phillip in the interim? And what did it have to do with Eden? More questions. More damn questions.

"Well," she said, snapping herself back to the present. "What now, Colonel? This is approximately where John found the unicorn."

Okay, Eden, he thought. They'd tackle her ghosts later. But he wouldn't wait much longer.

"I was hoping to be able to see the ground," he

said, "and check for signs John might have missed. But the snow took care of that plan. We'll head on up and look at the abandoned cabins. I know John did that, but humor me." He reached down for the tarp.

"Did you hear something?" Eden asked.

He looked up at the sky. "The chopper is coming in. Damn, I wish I had some way to communicate with that pilot. If he spots something, I won't know until I get back to the phone at your place. This operation is less than efficient, but it's the best we can do at the moment. Let's go."

They set out again on horseback, the climb up the slope slow and tiring. Eden directed them to the first cabin, and Mark told her to stay put while he checked it out.

"Nothing," he said, swinging back into the saddle. "Now where?"

"Up and to the left, then the third one is higher yet."

"Lordy, this is fun," he said dryly. "Don't say I don't take you on exciting dates, kid. This is thrill-a-minute time."

She laughed and nudged her horse forward.

The second cabin was also empty, with no sign that anyone had been there. They rode on.

"You know," Mark said. "John must have just opened the doors of those cabins and looked in. I went inside and my footprints are in the dust on the floor. There were no other tracks. I suppose he got the job done, but I'd have thought he'd be a little more thorough." He paused. "No, forget that. I'm being picky. The guy had a lot of ground to cover. Bill was either in the cabin, or he wasn't."

"And he wasn't," she said. "So, where is he?"

"I wish I knew." He rubbed his hand over his chin. "I hope I didn't screw up about those unicorns."

"What do you mean?"

"I don't know now which one was found out here, and which was in the shaving kit. If the order of those initials was important, I blew it."

"Anna Becker," Eden said. "Anna. We saw unicorns with an *N* and an *A*. I'm convinced that Bill had them made for Anna. But where is *she*? This is confusing. I'm not very good at this stuff."

"At the moment, I'm not doing a terrific job myself. It's still all a jumbled puzzle. But"—he shrugged—"puzzles can be solved with time and patience. And brilliance, of course."

She laughed. "Your arrogance is showing, Colonel."

"That's confidence, my dear, and a great deal of bull."

His horse stumbled, and his knee ached at the sudden jolt. "Lord, this is steep going here. This poor horse is earning his keep today, that's for sure."

The horses lunged up over an incline to a flatter stretch of land, and Mark pulled in his reins.

"Let's give these guys a breather. I can see the outline of the third cabin through the woods there. We'll walk in, okay?"

"Sure."

"I really don't expect to find anything in that cabin," he said. "We'll have lunch inside, though, while we're there."

They walked slowly through the trees, the horses plodding along behind them. Mark limped slightly, but Eden didn't comment, somehow knowing he wouldn't appreciate any more references to his knee.

"That cabin looks bigger than the others," he said.

"It is."

"Why are the cabins abandoned like this?"

"They've been here a long time. The people who built them couldn't use them after Henry Foster bought the land. This is all Lazy L property on this side of the ridge. I left the cabins standing in case hunters needed to take refuge. There's no hunting allowed in this section, but they pass through here. Oh, my feet are cold. Why doesn't that cabin seem to be getting any closer?"

He smiled at her. "Where's your patience?"

"Ask my frozen toes. I—"

"Hold it," he said, raising his hand. He stopped and pushed his Stetson up with his thumb.

"What is it?"

"Look at the snow over there," he said, pointing off to the side. "It's disturbed, not smooth like the rest. See? It's feathered as if something has been dragged over it. If you look closely you can make out a distinct trail from those trees toward the cabin. I think— Yes, someone was here, someone who pulled a branch with leaves behind him to cover his tracks. Recently too. These are the drifts from last night's storm. The earlier snow wasn't that heavy."

"This is getting a tad scary," she said.

"Well, one thing is for sure. We're not strolling up to the front door of that place like neighbors asking to borrow a cup of sugar. We'll tie the horses to a tree, you stay with them, and I'll go have a look."

"No. I want to come with you, Mark."

"Not a chance." He looped his reins over a branch and drew the rifle out of the boot of the saddle. "Stay right here. I won't be long. There's no smoke coming from that chimney, so I'd bet that cabin is as empty as the others. This is my 'better safe than sorry' routine. Do a tap dance to warm up your toes while I'm gone."

"But, Mark, what if someone—"

"Shh." He gave her a hard, fast kiss. "I'll be right back."

"Please be careful."

"Count on it." He moved off into the trees.

"Please, please, please, be careful," she whispered. She couldn't bear it if something happened to Mark. He'd come back to her safe and sound. He had to because . . . Because she was in love with him? No, she couldn't think about that now. She was too frightened for Mark. Oh, please, Mark, she begged silently, be careful!

Mark slipped through the trees, bending over slightly as he kept glancing at the cabin. He'd approach it from the side, he decided, and see if he could peer in a window. Whoever had been around and had covered his trail was probably long gone. But then again, maybe not.

He suddenly realized that this unknown person must have covered his tracks because he'd known Mark and Eden would be in the area, even though the sheriff's patrol had been there the day before.

He stopped at the edge of the trees. A thirty-foot clearing separated him from the front of the cabin.

"Wonderful," he muttered.

There was no indication that anyone was in the cabin, and the silence had an eerie quality to it, as if something just wasn't right. Thirty feet. Damn, that was thirty feet of being a sitting duck. Forget the plan to sneak up from the side. The cleared area surrounded the entire cabin, making any approach as bad as the next.

A sudden flash of light caused him to snap his head up to look at the rise beyond the cabin. The strange flash of light came again, and he squinted, trying to see through the trees in the distance.

He took one step forward.

He heard the crack of the rifle and felt the bullet slam into his right shoulder at almost the same instant. Before the message of white-hot pain reached his brain, raging anger filled him.

"Dammit!" he yelled, staggering backward into the cover of trees. "I'm sorry, Eden!"

Get one full-length Loveswept FREE every month!
Now you can be sure you'll never, ever miss a single
Loveswept title by enrolling in our special reader's home
delivery service. A service that will bring you all six new
Loveswept romances each month for the price of five—and
deliver them to you before they appear in the bookstores!

Examine 6 Loveswept Novels for

15 days FREE!

(SEE OTHER SIDE FOR DETAILS)

Six

For a horrifying moment after the sound of the rifle shot reverberated through the silence, Eden felt frozen in place, unable to move, to breathe, even to think clearly. A scream of fear caught in her throat.

In the next heartbeat, she gasped, her eyes wide with terror. *Mark! Oh, God, Mark!*

She grabbed the rifle from her saddle and took off at a run in the direction he'd gone, the roar of her pounding heart rushing in her ears. She tasted fear as she stumbled through the snow, oblivious to the branches dragging at her jacket. She was hot and then cold as she raced on. One image, one thought, beat against her mind. Mark.

She crashed through the trees and saw him.

He was on his back in the snow. His Stetson was a few yards away. His eyes were closed. His left hand covered his right shoulder, while his other arm was flung out at his side. His rifle was half-buried in a snowdrift beneath a tree.

"Mark," she whispered. She sank to her knees beside him, laying her rifle on the ground. "Mark? Oh, please, open your eyes. Mark, it's me, it's Eden."

To her horror, bright-red blood began to seep between his fingers where his hand lay on his heavy jacket.

"Oh, God." She placed her hand on the side of his face. "Mark. Mark, it's Eden. Please. Can you open your eyes?"

Mark heard Eden's voice calling him from a far-away place, a place on the other side of a wall of hot pain. He had to get to her! She needed him, he knew she did, and he had to struggle against the dark cocoon that held him. He had to fight his way through the haze of agony to reach her.

He was cold, and yet there was a warm moistness spreading across his chest. He fought a wave of dizziness that tried to drag him back into the darkness. He felt weighted down, unable to move or open his eyes. But he had to figure out what was wrong with him, because Eden needed him.

Cold. The snow. Yes, the snow. The warmth beneath his jacket was . . . was blood because . . . The sound of a rifle being fired . . . Yes, that was it. He'd been shot! The woods, the cabin, Eden. He had it all now, and somehow he'd find the strength to open his eyes and tell Eden not to be afraid.

"Mark?" she said, her voice trembling.

He concentrated, fighting against the pain and the grasping fingers of darkness, and opened his eyes halfway.

"Oh, thank heaven," she said. "Mark, can you hear me?"

"Mmm." He opened his eyes farther.

"Listen to me, please, listen. You've been shot. I've got to get you out of this snow. Do you know if someone is in the cabin? Did the shot come from there?"

"No," he mumbled. "Hill."

"Then we've got to get you into the cabin, okay?" She glanced at the open area, then at the hill. "Oh, Lord, what if he's still up there? We'll be right out in the open. We'll have to risk it. Mark?"

"Risk it," he said weakly. "Can't stay here. Get me up, Eden." He blinked, trying to clear his blurred vision. "Get me up, then stay in the cover of the trees until I get to the cabin."

"The hell I will, Mark Hampton," she said, tears clouding her eyes. "Just shut up and concentrate on getting to your feet."

"Eden . . ."

"Shut up, shut up." She nearly choked on a sob.

She slid one arm beneath his shoulders and grabbed the collar of his jacket with her other hand.

"Up, Mark. Come on."

With a groan, he came to a sitting position. Black dots swirled before his eyes. He began to tilt sideways, but she tightened her hold. He heard his rough breathing as if it were coming from a faraway place, heard the thudding of his heart as though it had moved outside of his body.

"Good," she said. "Now, up on your feet. Up, Mark. You've got to help me because you're too heavy. Are you ready?"

"No."

"Yes!"

"Okay, okay," he said, and surged upward. He

heard a moan, foggily realized it had come from him, and managed to stand. He swayed unsteadily, then began to topple over.

Eden slung her arms around his waist. "Don't fall. I'll never get you up again. It's not far. Just take small steps."

"Can't."

"Yes, you can." She breathed heavily as she supported more of his weight. "Move. Right now. Do it."

"You're crabby, Eden," he mumbled, starting forward.

"Just keep going. We'll discuss my mood later. The rifles . . . No, I can't get them now. That's it, keep going. The cabin isn't far."

They moved slowly across the clearing. Eden glanced only once at the hill above the cabin, then she tamped down her fear as she concentrated on Mark. Another groan rumbled up from his chest.

"Don't pass out on me now," she said. "We're almost there. Do you hear me?"

"Don't yell."

"Then keep moving!"

"Crabby."

"Oh, Mark, shut up."

"Mmm."

Step by slow step they covered the distance to the cabin. At last, Eden reached out a shaking hand and opened the door. She tightened her hold on Mark's waist and steered him inside. After kicking the door shut with her foot, she propelled him to the kitchen.

"Sit in that chair," she said. "Easy now."

He sank onto it heavily, his breathing as labored as hers, his chin dropping to his chest.

"We did it," she said, gasping. "Oh, Mark, we did it."

He slowly lifted his head. His eyes were cloudy with pain. "Thank you," he said, then clutched his right shoulder. His bloody fingers inched upward, and he cringed as he moved his hand to his back. "Bullet went through. Good. Damn, he ruined my favorite jacket."

Her eyes widened. "You're bleeding to death, and you're worried about your jacket?" she asked shrilly.

"I like this jacket," he said, sounding about four years old. "Why do you keep yelling at me? I really don't feel very well, Eden."

"Oh, Mark, I'm sorry." She blinked back a fresh flow of tears. "I was so scared when I heard the shot and . . . I'm still scared because I have to help you, and I don't know what to do, and you're bleeding, and . . ."

"Hey, I'm alive. Everything is going to be fine. It is, Eden, really. Help me out of this poor beat-up jacket, okay?"

"Yes. Yes, of course." She tugged the zipper down and he stiffened. "Oh, I'm sorry. I didn't mean to hurt you."

"Go ahead. I'm soaked through from the snow. I've got to get out of these clothes."

Her hands trembling, she worked the heavy jacket down his arms. She pressed her lips tightly together when she saw the dark stain of blood clearly visible even against his black flannel shirt. She dropped the jacket onto the floor.

Mark reached for the buttons on his shirt.

"I'll do it," she said.

"All right." He glanced around the room. "It's clean

in here, and totally furnished. The other cabins were empty. Ow!" he said as she pulled the shirt free of his jeans.

"Sorry." She eased the shirt down his arms. Beneath it was a heavy thermal top.

"You'll have to cut that off," he said. "I can't lift my arm."

She riffled through the drawers until she found a pair of scissors. Nervously, she cut from the hem to the neck, then carefully peeled the top away. "Oh, Mark, it's . . . Oh."

He turned his head to look at the ragged tear in his shoulder. It was swollen, and a dark bruise was beginning to spread beneath the skin. Blood trickled from the wound in a steady stream. His fingers probed his back, feeling where the bullet had passed through his body. A buzzing noise roared in his head, and he swayed in the chair.

"You have such a magnificent chest," Eden said, and giggled.

He looked up at her quickly. "Are you going to faint, Eden?"

"I beg your pardon?" she asked dreamily.

"Wonderful. We can . . . both pass out . . . on the floor."

"What?" She blinked once, then again. "Oh! I'm all right. I just phased away for a moment. Mark, you'll have to tell me what to do. That wound has to be tended to, you can't keep bleeding, and . . ." She glanced around. "Look, there's a small butane stove. I can heat water. You know someone has been staying here. There are dishes in the sink, trash in the basket. I thought John said . . . No, that's not important at the moment. Mark, tell me what to do to help you."

"Okay, just listen a minute. I'm going to pass out, and I can't postpone it much longer. I need to get dry and warm. Then you'll have to wash off . . . the wound, front and back, and try to . . . stop the bleeding . . . with cloths, rags . . . Understand?"

"Yes."

"Get me to . . . sofa . . . bed . . . something."

With his last strength he lunged to his feet. Eden rushed to his side, wrapping her arm around his waist again, and helped him across the kitchen. He closed his eyes as he forced himself to push one foot in front of the other. The trip was slow and exhausting, from the kitchen, through the living room, and into the bedroom. Eden ached from head to toe as she lowered him to the edge of a double bed.

"Hang on," she said desperately. "Just for a second."

"I'll try."

She ran into the bathroom and returned with an armload of towels. She folded one into a square and pressed it onto the wound on his upper back. He sucked in his breath.

"Okay." She pulled back the blankets. "Can you hold that towel?" He nodded and lifted his left hand to do as instructed. "I've got to get your clothes off before you lie down or the sheets will be wet." She pulled off his boots and socks, then reached for the snap on his jeans. "I don't suppose you could take your jeans off?"

"No."

She sighed. "That's what I thought. Can you stand up for a minute? I'll do this really fast, then you can rest. Okay?"

"Okay." He staggered to his feet. "But hurry up."

She shimmied the wet denim down his narrow hips, catching his long underwear and briefs with her thumbs as she went. Moments later, she eased a naked Mark Hampton onto the bed and covered him with the blankets. She folded another towel and pressed it onto the wound in front.

"Mark?"

"Hmm?" He didn't open his eyes.

"We did it. Rest now."

"Eden, I . . ." His head fell to one side.

She sank onto a rocker near the bed as her trembling legs refused to hold her for another moment. She was cold and wet, she realized. She had to get out of her own clothes and into something warm. Dear heaven, what a nightmare! Mark had been shot! Shot by someone who might still be out there, waiting and watching. But, no, maybe not. If he was still there, why had he allowed them to make it safely to the cabin? The cabin. She had to lock the doors and windows!

She ran frantically through the rooms, checking to make sure all was secure. Once more she sank wearily onto the rocker, only to rise again a moment later as she shivered. She had to find dry clothes. In the closet across the room she was surprised to discover several pairs of jeans and sweaters in different sizes. It was impossible to tell if the smaller things belonged to a woman or simply to a small man.

She glanced at Mark, who hadn't moved, then quickly shed her jacket, corduroys, boots, and long underwear. Her own sweater was still dry. The smaller jeans from the closet didn't fit, and the ones she pulled on were too long and had excess material at the hips, but they would do.

Pressing her fingertips to her throbbing temples, she told herself to calm down, to decide what to do and what order to do it in. First, Mark's wounds must be tended to.

She found a first-aid kit in the bathroom, then went into the kitchen to get a large bowl. To her amazement hot water ran from the faucet at the sink. The cabin, she realized, was in full working order. As she filled the bowl with water, her gaze fell on a stack of wood in a small utility room off the kitchen. But in the living room she saw the hearth was free of ashes.

Whoever had been there had not wanted smoke to be seen from the chimney. There were electric space heaters in both the living room and the bedroom, and, she surmised, the butane stove had been brought in to avoid lighting the wood-burning stove in the kitchen. Who had been there? Bill Johnson? And who had worn the small clothes? Where were these people now? Would they be back? Were she and Mark in danger because they were now in the cabin? It was all so frightening!

"Don't think about that part," she said. She turned on the space heater in the bedroom and sat down on the edge of the bed. Mark was important now, only Mark.

Without giving herself time to dwell on the fact that she'd never dealt with a gun wound before, or even seen one until now, she cleansed the raw area, patted it dry, then applied antiseptic and taped a thick gauze pad into place. She managed to repeat the process on the back of Mark's shoulder. He groaned once, but didn't open his eyes. She pulled the blankets higher onto his chest, then sat back down on the edge of the bed and stared at him.

He was so big and strong, a compelling man even now. She'd had only a fleeting glimpse of his nude body, but could see every inch of him clearly in her mind, including the crisscrossing network of scars across his right knee. His thighs and calves were like sculpted stone, covered with a smattering of dark hair. And his . . .

"That's enough, Eden," she said, feeling a warm flush on her cheeks. She brushed his tousled hair off his forehead, allowing the strands to glide through her fingers. He was so beautiful, she thought. And so very still. Was he sleeping, or was he unconscious? There had been so much blood soaking his shirts and jacket, but she had no idea if he'd lost a life-threatening amount.

Life-threatening? No. No, Mark was going to be fine. He'd survived that horror in Vietnam, and he'd survive this. *He was going to be fine!* And *she* was *not* going to fall apart.

She glanced at her watch and saw that it was nearly one-thirty. They were to meet John at three, and when they didn't show up, John and the deputies would come looking for them.

John knew where they had been headed and should have no difficulty finding them. Especially if . . . Yes, she'd start a fire. The people who had been here earlier might have wanted to keep their presence secret, but Eden certainly didn't. John, or maybe even the helicopter pilot if he flew over the area again, would see the smoke from the chimney.

And so would the man who had shot Mark.

She stiffened, then relaxed again. The man was gone. If he wasn't, she and Mark would never have made it from the woods to the cabin without being fired on.

Mark mumbled something, and she was instantly bending over him.

"Mark? Can you hear me?"

He was silent and she sighed, once again brushing his dark hair from his forehead. On impulse she pressed her lips to his, then straightened, blinking back unexpected tears.

"You're going to be fine, Mark Hampton," she said, her voice trembling. "Understand? Is that clear?" A sob escaped. "Please?"

Don't cry, Eden Landry, she told herself. She spun around and went into the living room.

A short time later, a warming fire crackled in the hearth, sending, she hoped, billows of smoke up the chimney for everyone to see. After scrubbing Mark's torn shirts and jacket, she draped their wet clothes over chairs near the fire. The cupboards in the kitchen were well stocked, and she heated soup on the butane stove. She ate while sitting in the rocker watching Mark. The horses, she knew, were fine for now. They were in an area sheltered by trees and were conditioned to the cold.

The rifles, she thought suddenly. They were across the clearing where she'd found Mark. Well, they were staying there, because she did not intend to put one toe outside the door until John Chambers came to get them. And he would come. Very soon. All she had to do was wait.

She finished her soup and set the bowl on the floor. Once again she checked Mark. His breathing was even and deep, and she prayed that meant he was sleeping peacefully. No blood had seeped through the thick gauze pads. She sank into the rocker and leaned her head back, realizing she was thoroughly exhausted, both physically and emotionally.

She closed her eyes and slept.

He was crawling, dragging his injured leg, but getting nowhere as the fire licked at his feet and seared his aching body. Closer and closer the flames came. Hot. So damn hot. He had to get out of there before he was consumed by the heat, turned into nothing but a pile of cinders. No one would know that he was dead, that the cinders had once been Mark Hampton. That was wrong. When a man died, his friends, his family, should know, should care, should see to it that kind words were said for his battered soul. He didn't want to be just a pile of cinders that no one would know was him. He had to crawl faster, get away from the fire, the heat. It was after him. Closer . . . closer . . .

"No!" he yelled, fighting against the flames. "No! No!"

Eden jerked awake, totally disoriented in the dark room. Where was she? she thought wildly. Who was— Oh, God, Mark!

She jumped to her feet, fully awake, her heart pounding. Groping in the darkness, she found the lamp on the nightstand and snapped it on, then glanced at her watch.

Six o'clock. It was after six o'clock and John hadn't come for them! She could hear the wind howling outside the cabin. The new storm had moved in, and—"

"No!" Mark yelled.

She stared down at him and gasped. He was thrashing on the bed, the blankets thrown far to the other side. His body glistened with perspiration, and fresh blood soaked the gauze pads. His eyes were closed, his features tight with pain.

She bent over and placed her hand on his forehead. He was burning with fever. She had to do something, had to help him. And she had to stay calm.

"No," he moaned.

"Mark." She grabbed his hands. "Can you hear me? Mark, it's Eden. Please lie still. You have a fever. I'm going to sponge you down, but you've got to lie quiet. You're bleeding again. Mark, listen to me. Please."

"The fire. The fire," he mumbled, tossing his head restlessly on the pillow. "Hot. So . . . damn . . . hot."

She ran into the kitchen and filled a large bowl with tepid water. Back in the bedroom, she lay wet towels on Mark's burning body, then replaced them one by one as they became too warm. For the next hour she made endless trips to the bathroom for fresh water, her arms aching from wringing out the towels. She changed the bandages and prayed the bleeding would stop.

A wicked wind hurled snow against the cabin, beating on the windows as though seeking entry to the warm, safe haven within. She hoped the horses had been able to pull the loosely tied reins free, then asked herself why she was thinking about horses when Mark was so very sick. Why hadn't John come for them? Why wasn't Mark's burning body getting any cooler? She was alone and frightened, and Mark needed her, but she wasn't sure she was doing all that should be done for him.

Stay calm! she told herself yet again.

Mark mumbled and cursed, shouted at a fire, raged in fury that he was going to die and no one would know.

She gently wiped his sweat-slicked face with a damp towel. "Shh, Mark, I'm here," she said. "It's Eden, Mark. I'm with you. There's no fire. You have a fever. Everything is going to be fine. Just lie still now and rest."

"Fire. Hot."

"Yes, I know you're hot, but it's not a fire. You're safe. You're with me, Mark, with Eden."

He groaned, but didn't open his eyes. "Eden," he said hoarsely, her name seeming to come from the depths of his soul.

"Yes," she said gently, wringing out the towel. "I'm here."

"Don't . . . leave . . . me. Talk . . . to me. Can't . . . crawl, the jungle . . . plane . . . Eden, don't send me . . . back there. Eden!"

"No, no, you're not in the jungle," she said, wiping his glistening chest. "You're in Montana. Did you know the word 'Montana' is derived from a Latin word meaning 'mountainous'? It . . . um, was admitted to the Union on November 8, 1889, and, I think, it's the fourth largest state."

A shudder ripped through Mark, then he quieted, no longer tossing his head on the pillow. She continued to bathe him, ignoring her aching arms as she talked on in a soothing voice.

"The average rainfall is fifteen inches, and the land area is more than ninety-three million acres. Isn't that a lot of acres? It certainly is. There are seven different Indian tribes living here. I've read all about them, and it's fascinating. Lots of people visit Montana every year. You're visiting Montana, too, Mark." She didn't notice the tears spilling onto her cheeks. "You're visiting, then you'll leave because that's what visitors do. You'll leave, and I'll hate that so much because . . ." She gasped for breath. ". . . because I love you and . . . Oh, dammit, Mark Hampton, I do love you so very much."

She dropped the towel onto the floor, covered her face with her hands, and wept. She cried because she was tired and frightened, and because Mark was hurt and she didn't want him to be hurt. She cried because she could no longer deny that she loved him, and because she knew he was going to have to leave. Wearing his uniform, he would leave her, and she would be so lonely. She cried because she wanted to, and the tears just kept on coming.

"Don't cry."

She snapped her head up and stared at Mark.

"Mark?" she whispered. She placed a trembling hand on his forehead. "You're cool. On, thank God, your fever has broken. You're . . . Oh, thank God." The tears started again.

"Hey," he said weakly, "don't do that. I can't handle your tears, Eden. Please don't cry. Why are you crying?"

She jumped to her feet. "Why am I crying?" she repeated loudly. "Well, I'll tell you, Colonel. In case you've forgotten, you've been shot. And John didn't come for us, and I don't know why, and you had a fever, and I've been sponging you down for fifteen years, and I thought you were going to die. I couldn't bear that, your dying, because I love you, and I really hate you because I've fallen in love with you.

And it's snowing. And . . ." She waved a hand in the air. ". . . And you lie there stark naked . . . And you can ask why I'm crying?" The tears continued to stream down her cheeks.

She loved him! Mark thought foggily. "Eden . . ." This beautiful, wonderful woman loved him! ". . . I . . ." And he loved her, would always love her. ". . . thirsty." What?

She blinked. "What?"

Dammit! he thought. There was so much buzzing in his mind, things he needed to say to Eden. Had he really managed only to croak out 'thirsty'?

"Thirsty?" she asked, bending over him. "Oh! Of course you are. Oh, my gosh. You've got to have liquids because of the fever. Don't go away. I'll be right back." She spun around and ran from the room.

"Wait," Mark called, attempting to sit up. Pain shot through his shoulder and he fell back against the pillow with a groan. "Dammit!"

He glanced down at his nude body and flipped the sheet and blanket over to cover himself. A smile tugged at his lips.

Eden loved him, he thought. She'd tended to his wounds and sponged him down until his fever broke. She must have been scared out of her mind, but she'd done it . . . for him. Nothing could stop them now. The future was theirs. Whatever obstacles, whatever walls, stood in their path, they would tackle them together. And he would tell Eden all of that if he could ever get his tongue to work.

She returned to the bedroom with a glass of juice.

"Here you are," she said, not meeting his eyes. "Can you sit up?"

"No. Need help."

"Oh. Well, okay." She set the glass on the night-stand, then slipped her arm beneath his shoulders. "Easy. Up you go." She pushed the pillow against the headboard and reached across him for the other pillow. "Hang on a second."

"Hi," he said.

She turned her head and nearly bumped her nose against his. Their eyes met and held for a timeless moment, then Eden tore her gaze away and whopped him on the head with the pillow before she stuffed it behind him.

"Ow," he said gruffly.

"Wiggle up there and drink this," she said, pick-ing up the glass.

He did as instructed, and she sat back down in the rocker. She rocked back and forth, staring at a spot on the far wall. He drained the glass.

"Thank you," he said, holding out the glass to her.

She set it on the nightstand. "You're welcome. Would you like some more?" She still didn't look directly at him.

"Maybe in a few minutes."

"Fine. If you think you're strong enough to sit in this chair, I could change the bed. Fresh sheets would feel better."

"Maybe in a few minutes."

"Fine. I guess we're stuck here for the night. I don't understand why John—"

"Eden."

"—didn't come looking for us. I have a fire going in case anyone is watching for smoke and—"

"Eden."

"No," she said, shaking her head. "I don't want to talk to you."

"Look at me."

"No."

"Eden, look . . . at . . . me."

Slowly, very slowly, she turned her head. She nearly began to cry again when she saw the warmth and love radiating from the depths of Mark's gray eyes.

"You love me," he said quietly. "And I love you more than I can ever begin to tell you. Don't be afraid of that love. We're going to be fine, you'll see. We'll work everything out together."

"I don't want to love you, Mark," she whispered. "I really don't."

"You can't turn it off once it happens. Eden, please, trust me a little. Admitting that you love me is the first step in tearing down those walls of yours. We'll do the rest together, you and me."

"You're here for now, Colonel," she said, lifting her chin, "but there's a uniform waiting for you back at the ranch, and with that uniform will come the orders. Men in uniform always follow orders. They go, not looking back, not seeing the tears being shed for them. I can't . . . I won't . . . do this, not again." She stood up. "I'll get you some more juice and a bowl of soup."

"I'm not going to lose you, Eden."

She looked at him for a moment, a sadness in her eyes, then turned and walked from the room.

"I won't lose you," he repeated quietly. "I can't. I just can't let that happen."

She returned with a tray, set it across his thighs, and sat back down in the rocker with a weary sigh.

"You're exhausted," he said. "You had a rough

time of it, taking care of me. I really appreciate everything you did."

"You're welcome." She leaned her head back and rocked slowly. "I wasn't sure if I was doing the right things for you. I just did them."

"It's not that serious a wound. The bullet went on through, the fever was pretty standard stuff. I'm just sorry you had to deal with it."

She lifted her head to look at him. "Did you see who shot you?"

"No. All I saw were a couple of flashes of light. Reflections off of something shiny, I think. Like maybe a . . ." He took a deep swallow of juice.

"A what?"

"A sheriff's badge."

She sat up straight. "What? What are you saying? You think *John* shot you? That's insane, Mark."

"Is it?" he asked, looking at her again. "You said yourself that he was acting strangely this morning. He knew exactly where we were going to be. John has a badge on his shirt *and* his jacket. The deputies have only cloth emblems. And, Eden, I was shot before I got to this cabin. Why? Because John Chambers didn't want me to see inside and realize that it hasn't been empty for long, which is not the way he reported it. He indicated this place was as abandoned as the others."

She shook her head. "No, I can't believe John is involved in this."

"Then where is he? Why didn't he come looking for us?" He paused. "What time did this storm hit?"

"I don't know. I fell asleep. I hope the horses are all right."

"The reins weren't tied that tightly. I imagine they

pulled free, which means we're really stranded. When too much time passes and General Meyers can't reach me at your place, he'll send people in to find us. We'll just have to wait it out."

"Mark, John is a decent man, a good person."

"Well, things aren't adding up in his favor at the moment. I need to look around this cabin for clues, but I feel as weak as a baby right now."

"Eat your soup."

"Yes, ma'am," he said, smiling at her. Lord, how he loved her, he thought. But he wouldn't push her about it now. He'd put it on hold until they were safely out of this mess.

"Mark," she said, "there has been more than one person staying here. I found these jeans in that closet, and there's another pair there that are too small for me. There was a chili can in the trash and several bowls with traces of chili in the sink. There are space heaters and a butane stove, which is why they didn't have to light any fires and send up any smoke. The electricity is on, there's hot water . . . Everything was prepared for their arrival, including enough food for a week or so."

He smiled. "You're after my job again."

"No, thank you."

"So, okay, it's a very organized operation. Question. Who organized it? Question. Is Bill Johnson selling out, or was he kidnapped? Question. If Bill is innocent, who fine-tuned the timing of the finishing of Project Unicorn and getting Bill up here before he put the information in the master computer? Question. Where does Anna Becker fit into all this? And what about the silver unicorns?"

"And John?"

"Yes, and John. Is he involved?"

"No."

"You don't know that for sure."

She threw up her hands. "We don't know anything. All we have is a long list of questions."

"We do know we're here for the night. Where are the rifles?"

"Outside in a snowdrift."

"Are there any weapons in the cabin?"

"Not that I've seen."

"Are the doors locked?"

"Yes, and the windows."

He handed her the tray. "There, I ate every bite. Thank you. Eden, you're doing a fantastic job. A lot of people would have fallen apart by now. We'll get out of this and find all the answers to those questions. Just hang in there, okay?"

She sighed. "Okay. I'll go build up the fire in the living room.

As she left the room, Mark flipped back the blankets and eased his feet to the floor. He got up slowly, waiting for the dizziness to pass. On less than steady legs, he walked across the room to the bathroom.

When Eden came back to the bedroom she saw the empty bed, then the closed bathroom door. She quickly stripped the sweat-soaked sheets from the bed, and brought fresh linens from the closet shelf.

Mark shouldn't have gotten up alone, she thought, as she tucked the clean sheets into place. It would serve him right if he passed out on his face in the bathroom.

She stiffened. "Mark," she called, "are you all right?"

"Yes."

He'd say that no matter how he felt, she thought,

shoving a pillow into a pillowcase. Arrogant man. Magnificent man. The man she loved. Dear Lord, why? What had she fallen in love with him? And even worse, why had she told him about her feelings for him? She was an emotional wreck. She just wanted to crawl into bed and sleep for five years straight.

She smoothed the blankets just as she heard the bathroom door open behind her.

A naked Mark Hampton, she realized, was about to stroll across the room and get into that bed. So? She'd sponged down said naked body for an hour or more. Yet, the fact that he was now wide awake added a different element to the whole situation. Oh, for Pete's sake, she was a grown woman, not a child. She could handle this. Maybe.

"That bed looks terrific," he said from behind her. "I feel as though I've walked a mile, instead of across the room."

"Then get in there," she said, pointing to the bed. "Fast."

"Nice fresh sheets," he said as he walked past her.

Her gaze flickered over him. "You're wearing a towel. Isn't that nice? It certainly is. Towels are just so handy and . . Ignore me, I'm a basket case."

He settled into the bed and pulled the blankets up. "You're tired, Eden. Stretch out here next to me and rest. Believe me, you're safe in this bed with me tonight. I don't have the energy or strength to move. Come on."

"Well . . ."

He patted the expanse next to him. "Come on. You've had a helluva day."

"Maybe just for a few minutes."

"Sure."

She laid down, closed her eyes, and sighed.

"There," he said, "isn't that better?" He waited. "Eden?" He looked down at her. She was out like a light.

He smiled gently, then settled back onto his pillow, wishing the throbbing pain in his shoulder would go away.

They were in a terrible mess, he thought. He was too weak to move, there was little hope that the horses were still around, they had no weapons, and they didn't know the good guys from the bad. Not wonderful. All he could do was get a decent night's sleep—if the ache in his shoulder allowed it—and hope he was stronger in the morning. Then he'd have to come up with a plan.

In the meantime . . . His eyes drifted closed. . . . he'd . . . glory in the knowledge . . . that Eden loved him.

He reached for her hand, and slept.

Seven

Mark opened his eyes. Bright sunlight filled the room, and he quickly closed his eyes again.

In the next instant his eyes popped back open as one thought slammed against his brain. Eden. He turned his head and saw her sleeping next to him. She was lying on her side, facing him. Sometime during the night, she'd tugged off the jeans and her sweater and had crawled beneath the blankets, which were pulled up to her waist.

His blood flowed hot as his gaze skimmed over her. Her full breasts were covered with nothing more than a wispy film of lace, and her satiny skin beckoned to him to kiss it and touch it. Below the blankets would be those luscious long legs of hers, and probably only a scrap of fabric barely covering her femininity.

He was dying. He moaned as his body tightened with desire. He ached with the need to make her his, to become one with the only woman he'd ever loved. Her hair was an auburn halo on the pillow, and her lashes were fanned on her creamy skin. Her lips were slightly parted, as though inviting his kiss.

He rolled onto his left side to get a better view of the vision of loveliness next to him. His shoulder complained with grinding pain, but he ignored it. He lifted his hand to touch her, then let it lie on the blanket between them. The glow of love warmed and filled him, and tumbled together with the raging heat of his rising passion. His manhood stirred, full and heavy with need.

Eden lifted her lashes and looked directly into his eyes. He was sure his heart had stopped beating.

She blinked, then blinked again.

"Hello," he said, his voice husky with desire.

"Hello," she said, her voice sultry with the last traces of sleep.

"You're a lovely picture to wake up to. Really beautiful."

She glanced down at herself and gasped, then reached for the blankets to cover her chest.

His hand shot out to grasp hers. "Don't," he said quietly. "Let me look at you for a minute. You're exquisite, Eden, and I love you so much."

"I don't remember taking off my clothes. I was so worn out and . . . What I mean is, I didn't intend to strip down to my . . . Oh, never mind. How do you feel? How's your shoulder?"

"I probably need some stitches, but it's not bad, just throbbing like a toothache." His gaze slid over her body, concealed by the blankets. He swallowed heavily. "I want to touch you, Eden. I won't hurt you."

He slowly lifted his hand, waiting to see if she'd stop him. She didn't move, and her gaze was locked with his. He trailed his thumb over the curve of her breasts above the top of the blanket, and felt a tiny shiver course through her. His hand skimmed up to her shoulder, then down one arm. He lifted her hand and kissed each fingertip.

Heat pulsed deep within Eden as she watched Mark. His mouth was sweet torture, and she wanted more. She wanted all of him.

She loved him, and at that moment nothing else mattered. She didn't care where they were, or why they were there. She didn't care about the tomorrows and the tears they could bring. She wanted only now, only Mark. She loved him, and all other thoughts fled into a hazy mist beyond reality.

He lowered his head toward hers, and a tiny whisper of pleasure escaped from her throat as he covered her lips with his own. She filled her senses with his taste and aroma, with the feel of his hard muscles as she drew her hand down his arm.

The kiss deepened as their tongues met and dueled. Mark tossed the blankets away, revealing his aroused body and her scantily clothed one. He lifted his head, and his gaze played over her, not missing an inch.

As he looked at her, Eden, too, visually explored every part of him, marveling anew at his beauty and perfection. His body was hard and strong, his manhood a bold announcement of his desire for her. She felt no trepidation or hesitation. She knew only, as she had known all along, that this joining would be glorious, and so very right.

"Eden," he said, his voice raspy, "I want you so much."

"Yes," she whispered. "Oh, yes, I want you too. But your shoulder . . ."

"We'll . . . improvise. Are you very sure that you want this, that you're ready to take this step with me? No regrets? Please, Eden, be very, very sure."

"Yes. It's right, Mark. That's all I can say. It's right. I want to make love with you. I do."

With a groan, he claimed her mouth. His hand moved to her back and deftly undid the clasp of her bra. She shifted without breaking the kiss, and he drew her bra away and dropped it onto the floor. She felt the tremor in his hand as he cupped one breast in his palm, stroking the nipple to a taut button with his thumb. He slowly lifted his head to gaze at the bounty of her breasts.

"Beautiful," he said, "Beautiful."

He moved lower, again ignoring the shooting pain in his shoulder. His lips closed over one nipple, and he drew it deep into his mouth, laving it with his tongue, suckling, pulling, tasting, savoring.

She sighed with pleasure. The steady rhythm of his mouth on her breast was matched by a pulsing sensation deep within her. A wondrous trembling consumed her, and she moved closer, offering more, feeling his manhood surge against her thigh.

His hand moved lower, over the flat plane of her stomach to inch below the triangle of lace that covered her. An involuntary gasp whispered from her lips as his searching fingers found the dark, secret place of her femininity. Her body seemed to hum with joy as he stroked the very essence of her, and she arched upward against his hand. He gently slipped her panties down and away, then looked directly into her eyes.

"I love you," he said. "I don't want to rush you, but . . . Oh, Lord, Eden, I feel as though I've waited a lifetime for you."

She slid her hand across his chest, weaving her fingers through the dark curls, then moved lower, and lower yet.

"Eden!"

"I want you. Now. I love you, Mark," she said softly. "I need to say that. I don't want to think about it, I just need to say the words. I love you, Mark Hampton."

"Oh, Eden."

He circled her waist with his left arm and pulled her on top of him, stretching her out along his muscled body. He wove his hand through her silken hair to bring her mouth down to his for a hard, searing kiss.

"Improvise," she murmured against his lips.

"Okay?"

"More than okay. We're going to be wonderful together."

She slid slowly, sensually down, then sat up. Her knees were straddling his hips as she drew lazy pictures on his chest, his stomach, then lower. Mark sucked in his breath, his muscles tensing as he strove for control. His large hands gripped her waist and lifted her, then settled her over his burgeoning manhood. If there was any pain in his shoulder, he didn't feel it. He felt only Eden.

Her body sheathed him in silken heat as she received all that he was. Their eyes met in a moment too special and rare to be put into words. They were one. Meshed. Man and woman. Mark and Eden. A single entity.

Then she began to move. He lifted to meet her, to drive deeper within her. It was as tempestuous as the night's raging snowstorm. They gave and took as they searched higher . . . higher . . . higher . . .

"Mark!"

"Yes!"

He felt her tighten around him, spasms rippling through her slender body as she flung her head back, his name a litany chanted to the heavens. He surged upward one last time, spilling into her, feeling as though his entire body were being hurled into a nameless place.

She collapsed against him and he held her, their bodies still joined. Their labored breathing echoed in the quiet room. Slowly their heartbeats returned to normal, but still they didn't speak, savoring what they'd just shared. Eden sighed, a contented, sated sigh, and Mark smiled as he gently stroked her back. She pressed her lips to his neck and tasted the salty moistness of his skin.

"Incredible," he said.

"Wonderful."

"I love you, Eden."

"I love you, too, Mark."

Silence.

"It's as though," she said dreamily, "there's no world beyond this cabin. No, this room, just this room. It's peaceful here, it's ours, we're warm and—and safe."

Like the butterfly in the glass cube, he thought. No, Eden. Didn't she see how wrong it was to think of their relationship as being separate from the real world, as though it were protected by walls? Reality was beyond the door of the cabin, and they would face it, together.

Okay, he admitted to himself, first he had to get a sense of normalcy back into their lives. That did not include snipers in the woods, missing military computer geniuses, and mysterious silver unicorns popping up in unexplained places. It didn't include a long, frustrating list of unanswered questions. First things first, then. He'd finish this mess with Bill Johnson, then concentrate on Eden. Concentrate on making very sure he didn't lose her.

She wiggled against him, and his attention was immediately drawn from his worries back to the delectable woman in his arms.

"You feel so good." She trailed her fingers down his chest. "You make a nice pillow too," she added, pressing her hips tighter to his.

"Uh, ma'am?" he said, smiling at her. "You're asking for trouble there, ma'am."

"Me, Colonel?" She batted her eyelashes at him. "I'm only doing this." She moved her hips in a slow, sensuous circle. "And this." Her tongue feathered over one of his nipples.

He groaned in pleasure, feeling his manhood surge within her. "Deep, deep trouble." He lifted his hips.

"My, my, my, what is happening here?" she asked, a flush on her cheeks.

"What you started, I'm about to finish."

"Oh, thank goodness."

It was fast and rough. Their passions were kindled instantly from the glowing ember still within them to a hot flame. They made love again wildly, neither holding back as they searched for ecstasy. Crying out to each other in voices hoarse with desire, they spun away from the here and now, together. Lingered in a hazy place, together. Then drifted back and slept, together.

• • •

An hour later, Mark stirred, groaned as his shoulder delivered a sharp message of pain to his brain, and opened his eyes. Eden was curled up next to him, sleeping peacefully, and he kissed her lightly on the forehead. Back to business, Hampton, he told himself. As much as he might want to stay in this bed with her, they had to get back to the Lazy L.

He moved carefully off the bed, trying not to disturb Eden. In the bathroom, he managed a partial shower without getting the gauze pads on his wounds wet, then went in search of his clothes. They were dry but stiff, and his shirts were total disasters. He found a chamois shirt and a sweatshirt in the closet. They were slightly small, but adequate. Dressed, he walked into the kitchen to make coffee, then stared in amazement out the window.

"I'll be damned," he muttered.

Digging beneath the snow with their front hooves, searching for grass, were the two horses he and Eden had left tied to the tree.

"I'll be damned," he repeated, and headed for the bedroom.

Eden was just coming out of the bathroom wrapped in a towel. She stopped and looked at him, and all rational thoughts fled his mind. He strode over to her, captured her face in his hands, and kissed her long and hard.

"Hello," she said breathlessly, when he finally released her.

"Hi." He paused. "Eden, good news. Our horses are standing outside like waiting taxis. We're getting away from this place as soon as you get dressed and have a cup of coffee. I want to look around the rooms a bit." He turned and left the bedroom. "Hurry, okay?" he called.

No! she thought. She didn't want to leave here. It was their special place, their secret place, where no one and nothing existed but the two of them. Beyond this cabin were truths she didn't want to face. Beyond this cabin was a world of harsh reality that included a uniform belonging to Mark, a life that controlled him, would pull him from her arms forever. No!

"Eden," he called, "I've poured your coffee. Are you dressed?"

"What? Oh, I'll be right there," she said, as a wave of icy misery swept over her.

She retrieved her own clothes and after dressing found coffee waiting for her on the kitchen table. She saw no trace of Mark, though. He was outside, she knew, and a rush of fear clutched at her. He'd been shot out there. But, she reasoned, they couldn't stay holed up in the cabin. She wanted to, for more reasons than one, but life went on. It always did.

Mark came in the kitchen door and gingerly took off his torn Air Force jacket. He poured himself another cup of coffee and sat down opposite her at the table.

"Okay," he said, "here's the plan."

"Mark, you're in pain. I can tell."

He smiled at her. "Between the shoulder and the knee, I'm a terrific specimen. Listen, all right? I found the rifles, but they're soaked and not usable. I put them in the boots of the saddles so they'll *look* usable. The horses are fine, no worse for wear. We'll head back toward the ranch, but we're not going to ride in as though we've been on a Sunday picnic."

"Why not?"

"Because I don't know the players without a score-card, and I haven't got a scorecard. There's no telling what might be going on at the Lazy L." He shrugged, then wished he hadn't when his shoulder protested. "Maybe something, maybe nothing, but I intend to be careful. Ready to go? We should get to the ranch about two, if I don't have to rest often. We'll see how it goes."

"Yes, all right," she said quietly, staring into her mug.

"Everything is going to be fine," he said gently.

She looked up at him. "Is it?"

"I'll get this mess cleared up, then we'll concentrate on us." He raised a hand. "No, don't say anything negative about us, about what we shared here. We're going to sort through all the obstacles, toss out the ghosts, just as soon as we can. We have our whole future to plan."

No, they didn't, she thought. The moment Mark put on his uniform, the future they might have had together would go up in a puff of smoke. It would all be forgotten hopes and dreams.

"Let's go," he said, getting to his feet.

At the door, he kissed her. "I love you, Eden Landry."

She managed a weak smile and nod, then turned to pick up her jacket before he could see the tears shimmering in her eyes.

It was nearly four o'clock when Eden and Mark stood in the cover of trees on a rise above the Lazy L. To Mark's disgust, he'd tired easily, causing them to stop often and rest. As they'd made their way slowly down the rugged terrain, stopping occasionally to snack on the food in the saddlebags, his shoulder and knee had ached with increasing intensity. Now the ranch was within view, beckoning to them with their images of a warm fire, hot food, a comfortable bed.

"Damn," Mark said. "There's smoke coming from the chimney of the ranch house, and John's Bronco is parked in the drive." He ran his hand over his chin and frowned. "Well, all I can do is try to make my way to the house without being seen, and get a look in a window. There's an awful lot of open area, though. I hope the Sawyers don't spot me and decide to shout 'Howdy' at the top of their lungs."

"I'm going with you," she said.

"No."

"Yes. It's not up for discussion, Mark. That is my home, this is my land. There's someone in that house who has no right to be there, and I resent that."

"That someone, or someones, could be dangerous."

She pulled a rifle from the boot of her saddle. "I can be dangerous too."

"Eden, those rifles don't work!"

"The someones don't know that."

He rolled his eyes heavenward. "Oh, Lord."

"Have you got a better plan, Colonel?"

He sighed. "No. No, I don't. I'm not exactly in shape at the moment to get into a brawl with whoever is in there." He threw up his hands. "So, what do I do? I storm in with a phony rifle. Talk about a bunch of bull. This is ridiculous. And it's also the only game in town." He pulled the other rifle free, then turned to face her. "Eden, I don't want you in the middle of this. I don't know who's in that house, or why they're there. I love you, remember? How can you ask me to let you walk into what might be a lethal situation?"

"And I love you, remember? You're hurt, Mark. I realize I'm not exactly a highly trained Intelligence officer, but I'm better than nothing at this point. Let's go. My toes are getting cold again."

He brushed his lips over hers. "You're stubborn."

"I know. We established that fact already. Come on. Brother, are we going to feel stupid if no one is in there."

"They're in there. There's more smoke coming from the chimney now. Someone added more logs to the fire."

"Oh." Her eyes widened. "They're really in there, huh? Who?"

"That, my lovely partner in this insanity, is what we are about to find out."

They made their way down the hill. Mark limping badly as they bent over as much as possible. At last they reached a cluster of trees about a hundred feet from the side window of the living room.

"Now what?" Eden asked.

"Now, I get under that window, sneak a peek, then signal you when it's safe to join me."

"No."

"Eden, if I had my way you'd be up by the horses. This is what is known as compromise. You stay here, or so help me I'll tie you to that tree."

"With what?"

"Your corduroys."

"Oh. Well. I guess I'll wait here until you tell me to come."

He grinned at her. "Good idea."

"Mark, please be careful. Forget that. The last time I said it, you got shot."

He slid his hand to the nape of her neck, pulled her close for a searing kiss, then crouched low and headed across the open expanse as quickly as his knee would allow.

Eden watched, a tight knot of fear twisting in her stomach. Mark made it to the house, inched upward to peer in the window, then motioned to her to come. She kept low, as Mark had done, and was gasping for breath when she joined him.

"Bill is in there," he whispered. "There's an older man I don't recognize, and a young blonde woman too."

"Anna Becker?"

"Maybe. Eden, John Chambers is standing by the fire."

"Oh, no, not John. I was hoping he was out looking for us in the hills. Mark, maybe nothing is wrong. You know, they found Bill and . . . But why didn't John come for us?" She sighed.

"Until we sort this out, everyone is guilty. We'll go in the front door. Stay behind me. I hope it's unlocked. If I have to kick it in, I'll probably pass out. My biggest worry is that there could be other people in the kitchen, or wherever. Oh, well, there's no time to be picky. Everyone seems to be sitting around waiting for something. I'd like to have control of the situation before said something arrives. Okay, we're off. Stay low, under the windows. No, stay here."

"No."

"Didn't think so."

They moved so quickly that Eden had no time to

decide if she was too frightened to continue with her brave facade. They scrambled across the porch, Mark gritting his teeth against the pain jarring his entire body, then he reached up and turned the knob on the front door. In the next instant, he flung the door open and straightened, rifle at ready.

"Nobody move," he said, walking into the house.

Eden followed, her rifle firmly against her shoulder. "That's right. Don't move," she said, hoping her voice hadn't trembled. She kicked the door closed behind her.

"Colonel Hampton," Bill Johnson said, shock evident on his face.

"Bill," Mark said. "Colonel Kinney and General Meyers send their regards."

"Oh, thank God you got here in time, sir." Bill looked at the older man sitting by the fire. "I told you, you slime. I told you they'd never let you get away with this."

"Shut up," the woman across the room snapped. "I'm sick to death of hearing your voice."

"Oh, Anna," Bill said, "I thought you loved me. I thought . . . Colonel, it was all part of a complicated plan they had. They're foreign agents. Anna was assigned to get the computer program from me. She—she even moved in with me, said she loved me and . . . Damn, I was such a fool."

"Take it easy, Bill," Mark said. "I assume it was Anna's idea that you come up here for the weekend?"

"Yes, sir. She acted so concerned, said I seemed stressed out. She urged me to get away before I tried to put the last of the program in the master computer. I know, sir, that I was wrong to have told her about Project Unicorn, but I loved her, trusted her.

She brought home a brochure from this ranch and—
and here I am. They grabbed me when I went for a
ride. They had me in a cabin, then moved me down
here. I haven't given them one symbol of that program, Colonel. I swear I haven't."

"You will," the man sitting by the fire said calmly.
"You will."

"Sorry, chum," Mark said, "but this ball game is
over. You lose."

"No," a new voice said. "We've won."

"Jane," Eden gasped. "Fred. Dear heaven, what
are you doing?"

The older couple were standing in the doorway to
the hall, pointing rifles at Eden and Mark. Samson
stood behind them, his tail wagging as though he
were extremely pleased that so many people had
come to play with him.

"What are we doing?" Jane asked, a sneer in her
voice. "Being compensated at last for what was taken
from us. We were sure, so very sure, that Henry
Foster would leave this ranch to us in his will. We
slaved for that tyrant, worked from dawn until dusk.
And for what? Nothing. *Nothing!* We were left to beg
the great rich, beautiful woman from the big city to
allow us to stay in our home. We had to cater to
more rich people and their whims as they came here
to escape from their depraved lives. This ranch should
have been ours! But now we'll have money to go
away, buy our own place, live in the finest house
ever built. My daughter will see to it. Anna will see
to it."

Eden stared at Anna, then at Jane and Fred. "Anna
is your daughter? An enemy agent is—"

"Shut up!" Anna yelled. "Drop those rifles on the

floor. Now!" She stepped forward, and a flash of light glittered in the room.

"The light," Mark said. "The unicorns on that necklace you're wearing. You were on the hill. You shot me, Anna."

"Damn right, I did. I warned the deputies away by blowing off one of their hats. I was going back to the cabin to collect our things, and there you were, poking around. I should have killed you while I had the chance. I'm an expert shot. I only wounded you on purpose. Well, it's better this way. We can keep things tidy, dispose of all the troublesome people at once in an unfortunate fire that is going to destroy this house. Our helicopter will be here soon, and we'll be leaving. Taking with us, you understand, your stupid, gullible computer man. Now, drop those guns."

"Do it, Eden," Mark said, laying his rifle on the floor. "Put your rifle down." She did as he told her, her hand trembling.

"I don't like this, Jane," Fred said. "Nobody said nothing about killing people. Anna said we'd get lots of money if we helped her, but she didn't tell us we'd be doing any killing."

"Shut up, you old fool," Jane said. "This is our chance to be something more than just the hired help."

"You'd kill for money?" Eden asked. "Because your daughter got mixed up with the wrong people doesn't mean you have to. Jane, Fred, think about what you're doing!"

"Jane said this was good," Fred said. "She always makes the important decisions. Way back when, Jane said that Anna was to have the best, and we saved all our money to send her off to one of them fancy boarding schools, then college. Then one night, months ago, Anna came here to the ranch, said she'd been using the name Becker for several years, said she had a plan to make us rich. I didn't know about any killing people, though."

"It was a very well thought out plan," Mark said. "You people stop at nothing. You lived with a man, Anna, then involved your own mother and father in your scheme."

The older man by the fire stood up. "That's enough talk."

Mark shrugged. "Hey, what the hell? I hate unanswered questions. Can't hurt to let me have the answers since I won't be around to tell anyone. Who left the unicorn on the trail?"

"It came off my necklace," Anna said. "I like my necklace. Bill paid a lot of money for those unicorns."

"And the unicorn concealed in your shaving kit, Bill?" Mark asked.

"I was going to call Anna and ask her to join me up here," Bill said miserably. "The unicorn cost a bundle, so I hid it in the lining. I was going to surprise her with it. It had a *A* on it, and would have finished spelling her name. Oh, Anna, I loved you so much."

"Enough of that garbage," she said. "Where are my two unicorns? I want them."

"I have them," Mark said. "Well, I did, but they're up at the cabin. In fact, they'll raise some interesting questions when they're found by the military. They'll be coming, you know. You can't kidnap a captain and kill a colonel without upsetting the big brass. Those unicorns are going to trip you up."

Nice spiel, he thought dryly. The unicorns were right there in the pocket of his jacket. He was buying time, looking for a way to make his move. Where did John Chambers fit into all this? John was just standing there like a statue, not saying a word. And . . . he wasn't wearing his gun!

The older man pulled a gun from his pocket. "This nonsense is getting on my nerves," he said. "The helicopter is late. I want this finished." He pointed the gun at Eden and Mark. "Move over there by Bill."

"No," she said.

"Eden," Mark said, "there are now three guns pointed at us. This is no time to argue. John doesn't have a gun, and you'll notice he's being very quite and cooperative. Get it?" He gave her a hard stare. "That's how it's done."

John wasn't one of them, one of the bad guys, she thought wildly. That was what Mark was trying to tell her. The numbers were evening up, except they had guns pointed at them. There had to be a way . . .

"She's very stubborn," Mark said to the older man. "Eden and her dog have minds of their own." He shrugged. "What can I say? Some women are just harder to handle than others."

Dog? Eden thought. Samson? What did Mark want her to do with Samson? The silly animal was just standing behind the Sawyers wagging his tail to beat the band. *Standing behind the Sawyers.* Yes!

"Samson!" she yelled. "Peanut butter!"

In a blur of motion, total chaos ensued. Samson bounded full steam ahead between the Sawyers, knocking them both off balance. Fred struck his head on the edge of the door frame and crumbled to the floor. Jane was flung into Anna, and Bill flew into them with a body tackle. Mark lunged at the man holding the gun, and they fell heavily to the floor, the gun sliding free. John hurried to pick it up, along with Jane's and Fred's rifles. Samson wiggled in front of Eden, waiting for his peanut butter, as she stared in astonishment. Mark drew back his left fist and delivered as stunning blow to the older man's jaw. The man went completely still, his eyes closed.

"That's enough," John said, pointing the gun at Jane and Anna as they tussled with Bill. "Bill, move away. It's all over, folks."

Mark staggered to his feet. He could feel the fresh blood streaming down his chest from his wound.

"Eden?" he said, through a haze of pain.

She ran to his side. "Are you all right, Mark?"

"Yeah, sure, I'm fine." He smiled crookedly. "You saved the day, my love. We're buying Samson a case of peanut butter."

"Chopper coming in," Bill said, hurrying to the window. "Oh, hell."

"How many are we up against?" John asked.

"You guys are home free," Bill said. "It's General Meyers and Colonel Kinney. I'm about to be strung up by the thumbs. Hey, there's a trooper chopper coming in too. They're escorting an unmarked chopper."

"Damn you, that's our people!" Anna shrieked. "We were so close to our goal. I gave over a year of my life to this."

"And I," Bill said quietly, "gave all of my love to you, Anna. It's finished, all of it. You lost and, God help me, so did I."

Jane burst into tears. Anna gave her and Bill a look of loathing, then crossed her arms and stared at the floor.

"Bill," Mark said, "go meet the general before he tells those troops to surround the place. Keep that gun on these people, John, until the calvary gets in here."

"Sure thing, Mark."

Mark looked at Eden. "It's over. Everything . . . is going . . . to be . . . fine, just like . . . I said." He weaved unsteadily on his feet.

"Mark?" she asked anxiously. "Mark, what is . . ."

"Excuse me, ma'am," he said, and fell to the floor at her feet.

Eight

It seemed, Mark thought foggily, that since arriving in Montana he'd spent half his time waking up aching from head to toe. Well, that wasn't entirely true. There had been the fantastic times he'd awakened next to Eden.

He slowly opened his eyes, cringing as the bright sunlight flooding the room caused his head to beat like a bongo drum. He was in his room at the Lazy L, and it was morning, as evidenced by the sun, the stubble of beard on his face, and the rumble of hunger in his stomach.

"Oh," he groaned, pressing the heels of his hands to his temples. He'd like a word or two with that hotshot lieutenant that General Meyers had ordered to tend to his wounds. It hadn't been enough just to numb his shoulder while he'd stitched him up. He'd knocked him out cold with a needle big enough to use on a horse. After, of course, Mark had been hauled off the floor to give his report to the general.

Well, he mused, it was over. The assignment was wrapped up, the good guys separated from the bad, and everyone was happy, relatively speaking.

And now . . Eden.

He hadn't had a minute alone with her since he'd passed out on the floor. By the time General Meyers had left the ranch, Mark had been tucked into bed like a sleeping baby. He had to see Eden.

He threw back the blankets and sat up. It would be a toss-up, he decided, as to where he ached the most—his head, his shoulder, his knee . . . The hell with it. Taking a vote on his battered body wasn't going to help.

Half an hour later, he had showered, shaved, dressed in jeans and a heavy blue sweater, and felt there was a fighting chance that he might live.

He went in search of Eden and found her in the kitchen pouring herself a mug of coffee.

"Do you have another one of those?" he asked.

She looked up in surprise. "Mark! You startled me. I didn't expect you to wake up for hours."

He walked toward her. "I've already slept for hours." He accepted the mug she handed him, along with a plate of toast. "That yo-yo really knocked me out with that shot."

"He said you had to have complete rest, that your body had suffered a trauma."

Mark hooted with laughter and sat down at the table. "My body had suffered a trauma? I love it. Those guys are really into euphemism."

She sat down opposite him. "Seriously, how are you feeling?"

"My biggest complaint is the hangover from the shot. Did you see the size of that needle? How are *you*, Eden? I'm sorry I couldn't be with you last night. You had a lot to digest, and I wasn't around to talk about it, help you sort it through."

"I'm all right," she said quietly. "It was a shock, of course, finding out that the Sawyers were involved in this thing, but . . . Well, it's over now. Oh, General Meyers said you should call him today when you woke up."

"I'm not awake yet. You're the one I want to talk to."

She ran her fingertip around the rim of her mug, not looking at him. "Yes, I know you want to talk, but . . ." She lifted her head. "There's someone at the front door." She got up and hurried from the room.

"Damn," Mark said. "This place is a zoo." Samson came lumbering into the kitchen. "Hey, hero. Did the general give you a medal? A lifetime supply of peanut butter? You saved the day, champ." Samson wagged his tail as though he understood every word Mark was saying.

Eden came back into the kitchen with John Chambers.

"Hello, Mark," John said. "Could I speak with you for a minute? I owe both you and Eden an explanation."

"Here," she said, pouring him some coffee. "Sit down, John. Take off your coat."

And make it quick, Mark thought. He wanted to talk to Eden!

John settled onto a chair, a deep frown on his face. "Look, I feel rotten that you got shot, Mark. I should have been more alert, asked questions, pieced things together better. I did a lousy job during this whole thing, and I know it."

"No, you didn't, John," Eden said.

"Yes, I really did. I saw Fred Sawyer with a wagon-load of stuff up at that cabin some time ago. He said you'd decided to fix up the place, Eden, rent it out to hunters who wanted to stay higher in the hills before going over the ridge to hunt. I never asked you about it, then when I checked the place during the search, I just said it was empty . . . meaning Bill wasn't in there. I should have said something about that bigger cabin being completely ready to be used."

"You're being too hard on yourself, John," she said. "You thought I knew."

"John," Mark said, "up-front, okay? I get the impression you're not very happy with your job here."

"No, I'm not," John said. "I'm frustrated as hell because I can't get the equipment or manpower I need. I came home right after college to look after my folks. They were older, not in good health. After they died a few years back, I just stayed on. But I know now it's time for me to go. I'm going to send out some résumés, start looking around for something more challenging. I'm burned-out here, and it shows."

"Sounds good," Mark said. "You need a change."

"John," Eden asked, "why didn't you come looking for us when we didn't show up by the trucks on time?"

"I couldn't. The storm came in early."

"Oh, while I was sleeping. I didn't know that."

"I sent the deputies back to town, then decided to come here. I figured some military brass would call Mark, and I could tell them I needed help to find you. Nice plan, except I walked in on that joker, who pointed a gun at my head. They were all here by then, Bill, Anna Becker, the Sawyers, and that older man, Anna's controller. His name's Keatson, by the way. Anyhow, I just strolled in like an idiot, and they grabbed me. The rest you know. I'm really sorry."

"You didn't screw up, John," Mark said. "You were doing everything possible to get us out of the snow-drifts. Lighten up on yourself. You're a good search-and-rescue man. Whoever hires you somewhere else will have a real pro on his team."

John stood up and extended his hand to Mark. "Thanks, I appreciate that." Mark shook his hand. "I'll talk to you later."

"I'll see you out, John," Eden said.

After they left the room, Mark looked at the dog again. "John is A-okay, Samson. He's got a fine career ahead of him, wherever he goes. And now? I'm going to talk to Miss Landry." Samson thumped his tail on the floor.

But Eden didn't return to the kitchen. Mark drained his coffee mug, then strode from the room. He found her stripping the sheets from his bed. He leaned his uninjured shoulder against the doorjamb.

"Running, Eden?' he asked.

"I have laundry to do. I have to check the cabins, too, to see if they're ready for the next group of hunters. There's a man coming out from town to tend to the horses. Then I have to—"

"Stop it."

She dropped the sheets and spun around to face him. "What do you want me to say? General Meyers is waiting for your call, remember? He'll tell you how long they've decided you can have to recuperate from this famous trauma to your body, then he'll give you your orders to report back to Washington. You'll put on your uniform and go. That will be that. End of story."

"End? You and I are just beginning."

She shook her head. "No, we're not."

"Dammit, I love you, and you love me. We're going to work all this out together, like I said."

She grabbed a pillow, hugged it to her, and sank onto the edge of the bed. "No."

He crossed the room and sat down next to her. She stared at the pillow.

"Eden, don't do this to us. You're running farther and farther behind those walls of yours. Give us a chance. Please, talk to me, share, just like I did when I told you about Nam, about my wounded plane."

"No."

"Yes! Why are you here on this ranch? Why did you leave New York and all you had going for you there?"

She threw the pillow across the room as tears spilled onto her cheeks. "For Phillip! I did it for Phillip!"

"Your brother. Okay, we'll start there. Phillip was wounded in Vietnam. And?"

She drew a wobbly breath, then got to her feet. She walked to the window and stared out, and when she spoke again her voice was hushed.

"Phillip was on patrol when one of his friends stepped on a land mine and was killed. Phillip was badly injured. My father was over there too. When he heard Phillip had been hurt and was being flown out, he died. He never said a word. He just listened, then fell over dead from a heart attack."

"Lord," Mark said, shaking his head.

"My father was buried at Arlington, and they gave me the folded flag. I told you about the flags, didn't I? Yes, I did. I was just a kid, Mark. Then I flew to San Francisco to see Phillip in the hospital. They were trying to save his legs, and he had so many internal injuries . . . his kidneys were damaged. Months went by. Months, years. He was in and out of the veterans hospital there. So many operations, so much pain. He grew so withdrawn and depressed over those years. He could hardly walk and was in constant pain. They weren't sure how long his kidneys would function properly, and started talking about a transplant. Phillip was giving up on life, Mark, I could tell. My beautiful, laughing, wonderful Phillip was an empty shell."

"I'm sorry," Mark said quietly.

"One year went into the next, then the next. Finally, five years ago the psychiatrist who had been working with Phillip called me. He said that even if they found a matching kidney for Phillip, they couldn't operate with him being so depressed, just wanting to die. He was refusing to do the therapy for his legs. He—he just sat there. His kidneys were still functioning, but the doctors said their slow failure had put him into near critical condition. I had to do something. I bought this place and convinced Phillip I needed his help to run it. I walked away from my career and came here . . . for Phillip."

"Did he like it here?"

"At first," she said, nodding as she continued to

look out the window. "He started his therapy again, began talking about plans for the ranch. But . . ."

"Go on," Mark said gently.

"It didn't last. I'd see him watching the people, the healthy, happy people, then he'd look down at his legs. He used two canes to walk, and he still wasn't steady on his feet. He fell once in front of a group of people here, and screamed at them not to touch him, to go away and leave him alone. I was losing him, I knew it, and there was nothing I could do. My brother was dying before my eyes because he no longer had the will to live."

"Lord," Mark said. He went to her and pulled her into his arms, holding her as tightly to him as he was able.

"And he did die," she said, sobbing openly as she clutched his sweater. "We'd been here about two years. He went to bed one night and didn't wake up again. Before he went to bed he said, 'Sometimes a man just gets too tired to fight anymore. Just too damn tired.' That's the last thing he ever said to me. And then I had . . . I had two folded flags."

Mark felt his throat tighten with emotion as Eden cried in his arms. Dear Lord, he thought, what horrors she'd been through. And there he was, Colonel Mark Hampton, telling her that everything would be fine. Another man in uniform she could imagine as yet another folded flag.

"Why . . ." he started, then cleared his throat. "Why did you stay on here?"

"I was lost, confused, so unhappy. It took a long time to convince myself I'd done all I could for Phillip. I tortured myself with the thought that I could have done more for him. Finally, slowly, the inner peace came, little by little. I'd fallen into a quiet pattern of living and felt a sense of contentment. I just never went back to the life I'd known in New York. I had plenty of money coming in from the Eden products, and I just stayed here."

"I see."

She lifted her head to look up at him, tears brimming in her eyes. "Do you? Do you understand? I can't do it again, Mark. I love you, but I can't watch you walk away from me in that uniform. I'd always be wondering when they'd come to tell me that you . . . I can't do it again!"

He cupped her face in his hands. "It wouldn't be like that, Eden. I'm permanently assigned to Washington and—"

"No! For God's sake, Mark, if you're permanently assigned there, why are you here, why do you have a bullet wound in your shoulder? You have special training. The orders came and off you went. 'Yes, sir,' you said, and nearly got yourself killed here! I can't, I won't . . . No!" She pulled free and ran from the room.

"Eden!" he yelled. "Damn!" He kicked the leg of the dresser, and pain shot through his entire body. "Ow. Oh, hell." He sat down on the bed and stared up at the ceiling for a long moment.

Eden's walls were stronger than he'd realized, he thought gloomily. And the crummy part was, he really didn't blame her for the way she felt. All her misery was connected to the military, to the uniforms the two men she'd loved had worn. Now, she loved him, Mark, and he wore a uniform too. Only this time, she was going to run as fast and as far as she could from the potential, dreaded folded flag.

What in heaven's name was he going to do? How was he going to keep from losing Eden?

The telephone on the nightstand rang. He glanced at it, assuming Eden would answer it somewhere else in the house. On the fourth ring, he snatched up the receiver.

"Yeah, hello," he said gruffly.

"Mark? General Meyers."

"Oh, yes, sir. Hello."

"I just wanted to see how you were feeling this morning."

"The jury is still out." On a lot of things, he thought. "I'll live, I guess."

"Well, you certainly wrapped this Project Unicorn situation up very nicely. Take a few days off, then when you get back here, I'd like you to investigate the security clearance on all the projects presently in operation that were put into effect before you were assigned here."

Another thrill a minute, Mark thought. Boring as hell, actually. "Yes, sir."

"The President asked me to convey his personal thanks to you."

"Thank you, sir, but Samson the dog was the real hero."

General Meyers laughed. "You did a helluva fine job, Mark. This will look very good in your file. My concern is that the President will get it into his head to have you check out some of our overseas operations. I'd hate to lose you."

Mark stiffened. "I was told I'm on permanent assignment to Washington, General. Permanent. It was a perk I was given for taking on some real sleazeball assignments overseas."

"I realize that, but if the President decides otherwise . . . Well, time will tell. You're used to packing up and moving out. It goes with the uniform."

"Goes with the uniform," Mark repeated slowly.

"I hope it doesn't happen. I need you here. Well, relax, recuperate, and I'll see you in a few days."

"Fine. Thank you, sir. Good-bye."

Mark replaced the receiver, then stared at it, replaying in his mind everything General Meyers had said. It was true, he thought. At any given moment his "permanent" orders could be changed, and he'd be transferred to heaven-only-knew-where. It had never bothered him before. The military life had always suited him just fine. Until now. Until Eden.

He left the bedroom, knowing where he wanted to go, what he needed to see. A few minutes later he entered the library and went to stand by the fireplace, remembering his daydream of the roaring fire in the hearth, of Eden nestled close to him on the sofa, their children sleeping peacefully in their beds.

Now, he thought, he and Eden were alone. Alone to talk, to share, to fill their senses with the very essence of the other, their partner in life, their other half. Lord, it was good. And he wanted it, all of it, with his Eden.

And it was never going to happen while he wore a uniform.

He sat on the edge of the sofa and leaned his elbows on his knees, making a steeple of his fingers. He stared into the cold, empty fireplace, which suddenly seemed to represent his future if he went through his remaining days without Eden.

He'd had a fine life in the Air Force, he mused. He'd flown the planes of his dreams, had faced adventures and challenges most men would never know. He'd served his country well, and had kept the name Hampton something to be proud of. He'd worn his uniform with pride, and felt humbled by the honors bestowed on him over the years.

But he was tired.

And he was lonely.

And for the first time in his life he was in love.

He was at a crossroads, he thought, a time of decision that would have far-reaching ramifications. He had to solve the puzzle that suddenly represented his life and his entire future.

Was he capable, he wondered, of thinking clearly while he was so close to Eden? When every thought in his mind seemed to be of her, when the desire to pull her into his arms overshadowed everything else? Could he view objectively all he had to see and analyze, when his vision was filled with only her?

He stood up slowly and stared into the cold hearth a moment longer, then crossed the room to the desk. The crystal butterfly in the glass cube caught his eye. He ran his fingertip over the smooth surface of the cube.

"Keep your wings on, honey," he said quietly. "There's rough weather ahead, I'm afraid. Hang in there."

He wandered into the living room, put more logs on the fire, then turned to see Eden standing in the doorway, her cheeks flushed with cold.

"I'm sorry," she said softly. "I ran away like a child. I went to the barn, and didn't know why I was there. I just ran. I guess . . . maybe I've been running for a long time from . . ." She blinked back sudden tears. ". . . from life."

"Eden—"

"No," she said, raising a hand. "Let me finish. After—after Phillip died I could have gone back to New York, to the life I'd had there. It had been fun, exciting, and I'd enjoyed it most of the time. But I became obsessed with the need to feel safe, protected from anything that could harm or hurt me. I closed off my heart, I built those walls you've spoken of, because to love, as I'd loved my mother, father, brother, had brought me immeasurable pain."

"I understand," he said quietly.

"Then you came, chipping away at the walls, pulling them down, inch by emotional inch, and I fell in love with you. But, oh, Lord, Mark, it frightens me so terribly. I have no defense against the hurt, against that uniform you wear, the leaving and the tears it brings, the ache in my heart, the fear in my soul. No defense at all. I don't . . . know what . . . to do."

He nodded, feeling a pain within him that had nothing to do with his wounded shoulder or battered knee. At that moment he wasn't a person who wore a uniform, or a pilot, a colonel, or an Intelligence officer. He was simply a man. Stripped bare and vulnerable, he was a man, and the future was suddenly an unclear, hazy mass of confusion covered in a fog of doubts and unanswered questions.

"I think," he said, his voice thick with emotion, "we need some time, both of us, away from each other. So much has happened. We've got to sort it out. I can't do that while I'm with you, and I don't think you can do it while I'm here. I'm—I'm going back to Washington tomorrow."

No! She screamed silently. He couldn't leave her! He mustn't leave her! She loved him. She . . . Oh, dammit, he was right. She needed time, and she needed space. She couldn't untangle her jumbled thoughts while he was here. But, oh, dear Lord, she didn't want him to.

"I see," she whispered. "You're right. We need time. I don't want you to be right, but you are." She drew a shuddering breath. "Mark, would you make love to me, please? Now? I need you. Please?"

Unable to speak, he opened his arms to her. She ran into them, bringing all that she was as a woman, and receiving all that he was as a man.

There were no yesterdays, no tomorrows, there was only now.

Their lovemaking was slow and sensuous. In the glow of the firelight they became one in a joining that was beyond beautiful. They gave and took, demanded and received, held nothing back. Declaring their love, they were flung into the oblivion of splendor, then clung to each other as they drifted back. The flames warmed their bodies, their love warmed their hearts and souls.

Then, before reality could intrude on their private world, they reached for each other once again, keeping at bay everything that had to be faced later. There was only the two of them soaring, and soaring, and soaring . . . as one.

Nine

With the dawn came reality. The previous day, Eden and Mark had shut the door not only on the world, but also on their own inner turmoil. They had basked in the glow of their love. A mere glance, touch, smile, would bring them once again into each other's arms. Those were precious, stolen hours that they cherished and tucked away in private chambers of their minds, hearts, and souls.

But with the dawn came reality.

They lay quietly in each other's arms, not speaking. Then Eden slipped from the bed and went to her own room to shower and dress. Mark sighed, threw back the blankets, and got to his feet.

After shaving and showering, he tucked a towel around his hips and opened the closet door. He stared long and hard at his uniform, then with another sigh, reached in and pulled it free.

After her shower, Eden dressed in gray flannel

slacks and a white, embroidered sweater. She brushed her hair until it shone, applied makeup lightly, then drew a deep, steadying breath. She would not, she told herself firmly, fall apart. Yes, Mark was leaving, but he had to, she knew that. They needed this time apart to think through everything. There were so many questions that had to have answers, and she knew that. But she didn't want him to go!

She left the bedroom and walked down the hall, and the aroma of fresh coffee reached her. Mark was in the kitchen, she realized. She needed another minute alone before she could face him, force a lightness to her voice, and a smile onto her lips. She detoured into the library and snapped on the desk lamp.

Her gaze fell on the butterfly in the glass cube, and her eyes widened as a gasp of horror escaped from her.

"No," she said. "No!"

"Eden?"

She spun around and saw Mark in the shadows across the room, tall, massive, dark, wearing his uniform. He moved slowly toward her.

"Eden?"

"I—I don't understand what happened. Why . . ."

He put his arms around her, frowning as he searched her pale face. "What's wrong? What happened that you don't understand?"

"The butterfly," she whispered.

He looked at the cube, and his heart thundered in his chest.

The butterfly's wings had broken off and were lying in the bottom of the cube.

"It—it was supposed to be safe in there," she said,

her voice trembling. "Nothing could hurt or harm it. Nothing. But its wings are tattered. The butterfly is broken, Mark. It wasn't safe at all." She pressed her hand to her forehead. "I don't understand. This shouldn't have happened."

"Eden . . ."

"No, no," she said, backing away from him. "I have nowhere to put this in my mind. I don't know what it means. I can't think when you touch me. I've got to be alone. Oh, please, Mark, go, now."

"Not like this, not when you're so upset."

"Yes, you have to." She looked at the glass cube again. "Yes."

He lifted his hand to touch her pale cheek, but hesitated. Taking a step backward, he dropped his hand to his side. He felt cold, empty, like the fireplace across the room. Pain as sharp as a twisting knife coursed through his entire body.

He was losing his Eden. No!

He looked at the butterfly, frantically searching for something to say, for a way to explain the broken, tattered wings. But he found nothing.

"Please," she whispered again, still staring at the cube. "Go."

He turned, every movement agony, every muscle coiled and tense. He forced one foot in front of the other to cross the room. At the door, he stopped.

"I love you, Eden," he said, his voice husky with emotion.

She slowly shifted her gaze to him. Memories of years past slammed against her mind as through her tears she saw once again the uniformed back of someone she loved leaving her.

Mark left the room, and a minute later she heard

the quiet click of the front door closing behind him. She jerked as if struck, then dropped to her knees as her trembling legs refused to hold her for another instant. She covered her face with her hands and wept, her sobs echoing in the silent room.

The lamp light shimmered over the glass cube and the crystal butterfly within, its broken wings lying on the bottom.

And huddled on the floor, Eden Landry cried on and on as though her heart were shattering into a million pieces.

Mark looked up to see General Meyers entering his office.

"Don't get up," the general said, sitting in a chair opposite Mark's desk. "You're working late again."

Mark tossed his pen onto the file atop his desk and leaned back in his chair. He squeezed the bridge of his nose for a moment before looking at the general again.

"Yes," he said, "I have a lot to do."

"You look like hell."

"Oh, thanks." He laughed shortly. "That's always nice to hear."

"I think you came back to work too soon after being shot, Mark. Plus, you've been driving yourself to the edge in the two weeks since you've returned from Montana."

Mark's jaw tightened. "Like I said, I have a lot to do."

"Something happened to you in Montana."

"I was shot."

"Come on, Mark. Off the record, okay? You're like

a bomb ready to explode. You've got that twit of an aide of yours shaking in his shorts every time you walk in the room. Even Kathleen is worried about you. She told me you hadn't smiled at her since you got back, hadn't carried on with the nonsense you two engage in. It's as though you're here but you're not. Talk to me, dammit. What's going on?"

"Nothing."

"Oh? Then why did I get a call from General Blake saying one of my top officers, a certain Colonel Mark Hampton, is late in filing his re-up papers? Your present tour is over in two months. You'll have twenty years in. Paperwork takes time, you know that. Your request for another five or ten-year re-up is late. Why?"

Mark pounded the desk with his fist and lunged to his feet. "Dammit, get off my back!" He sighed and rolled his eyes. "That was terrific, Hampton. Yell in a general's face. I'm sorry, sir."

General Meyers chuckled. "I said this was off the record. I'd appreciate it if you didn't deck me, though." He became serious again. "What is it, Mark? Did something happen in Montana that I don't know about, or is it simply a case of your deciding whether to re-up or get out?"

Mark ran his hand over his chin, then moved away from the desk. Shoving his hands in his pockets, he began to pace the floor. Several minutes passed. General Meyers waited without speaking.

"Both," Mark finally said, continuing his trek back and forth across the small office. "Something . . . No, *someone* happened in Montana, and I know my re-up papers are late because I haven't decided what to do. The thing is . . ." He shook his head and frowned.

"Go on."

"I don't know how to do this."

"Do what?"

"Be in love."

General Meyers was silent for a moment. "Oh, I see," he said slowly. "There's no handbook on love, you know, Mark. You listen to your heart. Hell's fire, that sounds corny, but it's true."

Mark stopped pacing and looked at the older man. "Love is very confusing."

"That's no news flash. I've been married for thirty-six years, and it's still confusing at times."

"Thirty-six years," Mark repeated. "Whew. Well, that makes you a pro. So, you should have some of the answers I need."

"Don't count on it," the general said, chuckling.

Mark resumed his pacing. "Question," he said, pointing a finger in the air. "Do I go through the pros and cons of re-upping while thinking of myself as a single entity, or do I take Eden's feelings on the matter into consideration? Further," Mark went on, "if a man's priorities have shifted, if it's become more important to him to have a home than to stay with the military, and if he knows the woman he loves won't stand for him being in the military, should he choose not to re-up?"

"Well . . ."

"But, if you love someone, aren't you supposed to still be a total person when you're alone, have a sense of peace within yourself?"

"Well . . ."

"Of course, you are," Mark said decisively. "Otherwise, you're asking too much of the person you love, expecting her to make you whole. So! Do I, Colonel Mark Hampton, want to re-up in the United States Air Force?"

"Damned if I know," the general said, throwing up his hands.

"No, sir, I do not!" Mark strode over to the filing cabinet and gazed at the airplane model sitting on top of it. "And I knew that, really, before I even met Eden. I just hadn't stopped long enough to figure it out. I want to open a flying school, be an instructor, get back behind the controls of an airplane where I belong. And separate and apart from that, I want to marry Eden, have children with her, spend the rest of our lives together." He crossed the room, grabbed the general's hand, and shook it vigorously. "Thank you, sir. I can't tell you how much your help means to me."

"But I didn't . . ."

"Love isn't confusing at all, once you sort it out. It took you to show me that. You're a very wise man, General. May I have a seventy-two-hour leave? I need to go to Montana."

"Sure," General Meyers said. He appeared rather dazed as he stood up. "I'll be sorry to lose you, Mark, but I wish you all the best."

"I'm not home free yet, sir. There's a little matter of some tattered wings to clear up."

The General shook his head. "I'll pass on that one." He started toward the door. "Good night, Mark."

"Good night, sir, and thank you again."

"So, I'm a genius," the general said, shrugging. "I can live with that."

• • •

A half an hour later, Mark peered in the window of a small shop that was one of many in an exclusive section of Georgetown. As he opened the door, a bell tinkled and an attractive woman in her thirties looked up at him.

"Good evening, Colonel"—she glanced at the name tag on his uniform—"Hampton. How may I help you?"

"You specialize in crystal figurines?"

"Yes."

"I'm hoping you can answer a few questions for me. Suppose you make a special glass cube to protect a delicate, crystal butterfly. Then one day, for no apparent reason, the butterfly's wings break off and fall to the bottom of the cube. It's been sitting there safe from harm in that cube, and suddenly it's broken. Does that make any sense to you at all?"

"Absolutely," the woman said. "I can tell you exactly what happened."

Mark leaned his arms on the counter. "I'm listening to every word."

Eden sat on the sofa in the living room, staring into the fire. She was postponing going to bed, postponing facing another night of tossing, turning, and missing Mark.

She couldn't go on like this, she told herself. The ache in her heart grew more intense with each hour of every passing day. She was alone and lonely, the future stretching before her as an infinity of emptiness.

She'd sorted all the facts connected to her relationship with Mark, as she'd known she must do.

The truth was clear. She hated the uniform, she loved the man. She loved the man with every breath in her body.

The time had come, she thought, to make a choice. She could allow the past, with its pain and tears, to rule her future, or she could step from behind her walls, crush them and her fears, and share her life and love with Mark.

She drew a deep breath, lifted her chin, and got up from the sofa. In the library, she snapped on the desk lamp and sat down in the leather chair.

"You didn't keep your wings on, honey," she said to the butterfly. "Mark's plane didn't, either, but he survived because he refused to be defeated. Now, it's my turn to be brave, little butterfly."

She pulled on the desk drawer and removed a heavy letter opener. A moment later, the sound of breaking glass echoed through the room.

Eden carefully lifted the butterfly and set it apart from the shattered cube.

"You're free," she whispered, placing the broken wings next to the crystal figurine. "And I'm free."

With a sense of peace greater than any she had ever known, she left the library and walked down the hall to her bedroom. Within minutes after slipping into bed, she fell asleep . . . and dreamed of Mark.

Just before noon the next day, Eden set her suitcase by the front door, then walked into the kitchen to check once again the list she had made of everything that needed to be done.

John Chambers had recommended a retired couple from town who had once run an establishment like the Lazy L. They had agreed to come to the ranch late that evening and take charge for a week. Eden had written out detailed instructions, including the fact that Samson should be given a spoonful of peanut butter daily.

One week, she mused. Seven days to convince Mark that she did love him, and that she'd gathered her courage and beaten the ghosts of her past. A measured number of hours to show him she was no longer living behind walls or inside a glass cube.

But what of Mark? she wondered. What answers had he come up with during the two weeks they'd been apart? Did he still love her, did he still want her in his life? Or had he discovered, once he'd returned to his world, that she had been nothing more than a mistake in judgment?

She had to find out, she thought, and she was going to him now. Soon she would learn the answers to what the future held.

A knock at the front door brought her from her tangled thoughts, and she hurried from the kitchen. In the living room, she opened the door, then just stood and stared at Mark.

"Hello, Eden," he said quietly. "May I come in?"

She blinked. "What? Oh! Yes, of course." She stepped back and he entered. She closed the door, her gaze never leaving him as he shrugged out of a new Air Force jacket.

Mark, she thought. Magnificent Mark, in jeans and a white fisherman's-knit sweater. Mark, the man she loved, was standing in her living room!

He turned to face her, and his jaw tightened when he saw the suitcase by the door.

"Going somewhere?" he asked, his voice ominously low as he met her gaze.

"Yes, I—"

"Running isn't the answer, Eden. I was hoping you'd realize that during these two weeks."

"Oh, but, I—"

"Do you mind if I sit down?" Without waiting for an answer he strode across the room and sat in the chair by the fireplace. She sat on the sofa, looking at him anxiously. "I came here to talk to you, Eden. It appears that I nearly missed you since you're obviously leaving."

"Mark, you don't understand."

"I think I do," he said, no warmth in his voice. "You had your life all figured out. This ranch"—he swept a hand in the air—"was your protective glass cube, your place to be safe from hurt or harm, just like the crystal butterfly. Then I came. And we fell in love. Love was threatening to you, because everyone you'd loved in the past had left you."

"Yes," she said, "that's true."

"Our love frightened you, didn't it? You wanted me, what we could have together, but you were scared. Then, the butterfly broke. When you saw those broken wings, you felt it was an omen, a sign that you were making a terrible mistake by loving me."

"I didn't know what to think," she said, her voice rising. "I was awfully confused."

He leaned forward. "Eden," he said softly, "I know why the butterfly's wings broke. I went to an expert and asked."

"It shouldn't have happened. The butterfly was protected in that cube."

"No. Listen to me. Glass has invisible stress points. It may be fine forever, or there may be leakage through those points. Keeping that butterfly in the cube, behind those walls, couldn't prevent what happened. Keeping yourself behind walls isn't going to solve anything either. Life is for living, for loving, but there are no guarantees. Sometimes you have to take a chance, lay it all on the line."

"Mark, I—"

He raised a hand to silence her. "Let me finish. Wouldn't you rather be free, like a real butterfly? Wouldn't you be happier in the sunshine, with me? I'll do everything within my power to make you happy, to keep you safe, but I can't predict what will happen. Don't you see, Eden? Living behind walls isn't a haven of protection, it's a sentence of loneliness. I love you. I want you with me, as my wife, the mother of my children. I want to spend the remainder of my days with you."

Tears spilled onto her cheeks, and she dashed them away as she continued to stare at Mark.

"I know how you feel about my uniform, my military career," he went on. "During the past two weeks I've tried to solve the puzzle of all I was feeling. Then, at last, I found the missing piece. I had to step away from the thoughts of you, from the ache of missing you, and discover what I, Mark Hampton, wanted to do with my life. Only then could I love you as you deserve to be loved."

He drew a deep breath and let it out slowly.

"Eden, I'm retiring from the Air Force in two months when my enlistment is up. I'm doing it for me, because I have dreams of being a flying instructor. I'm sorry if it hurts you to hear that I'm not leaving the military for you, for us, but I had to do it this way. I had to do it for myself before I came back here to you."

He stood up and paced the floor, then stopped in front of her.

"Came back to find," he said, pain evident in his voice, "that you're still running." His glance flickered over the suitcase by the door, then he looked at her again. "I'm losing you, and I don't know how to keep it from happening." He drew a shaking hand down his face. "Eden, I love you so much."

She jumped to her feet, unable to halt the tears streaming down her face.

"Oh, Mark, I love you too. I do! I was running to you."

"What?"

"I conquered my ghosts, Mark. The past was controlling my life, robbing me of a future with you. I was coming to tell you how much I love you, and that I wanted to be a part of your life—a life I knew would include your wearing a uniform. I broke the glass cube and set the butterfly free, and I freed myself at the same time. I, too, was coming to you as the woman I was meant to be. Free to live, and free to love . . . you, only you."

With a strangled groan, he pulled her into his arms. He held her close, burying his face in her silky, fragrant hair. She wrapped her arms around his waist, savoring his strength, his heat.

"Oh, thank heaven," he murmured.

He lifted his head and kissed her. It was a kiss of commitment, of answers found, of promises for the tomorrows they would share. It was a kiss of want and need, speaking of the painful uncertainties of the last two long, lonely weeks, now to be forgotten. It was a kiss of love.

When he raised his head, his breathing was rough. "I love you."

"And I love you."

He smiled at her. "Want to strike a deal?"

"Well, that depends on the deal," she said, matching his smile.

"We'll add flying lessons to your dude ranch agenda in the summer. But! We close this place up and go to a warm climate in the winter. Some pilot buddies of mine have a flying school in Texas, and they've offered me a spot. My poor battered, war-wound knee can't handle these Montana winters. In exchange—"

"Yes?"

"I'll supply Samson with a lifetime stash of peanut butter."

She laughed in delight. "You've got yourself a deal, Colonel."

He became serious again. "Not Colonel, just Mark. Just the man who loves you more than I have words to tell you." He paused. "Maybe . . . I don't know . . . maybe you want to do some modeling for Eden products."

"Nope. I'll be too busy being your wife, helping to run this place, and waddling around pregnant."

"Pregnant?"

"You did say you wanted children, didn't you?"

"Well, yes, but . . ."

"Then I think we should get started on that project, Mister Hampton."

"Oh, lady, I like the way your mind works."

"Come with me, my love," she said, taking his hand. "I've missed you so much, Mark."

They started across the room, and Mark chuckled softly. She looked up at him questioningly.

"I was just thinking," he said, "that from here on there will be no such thing as a crummy Monday. Not as long as we're together."

She smiled warmly at him, her eyes radiating messages of love as they continued down the hall to the bedroom.

In the library, the crystal butterfly sparkled in the glow of the desk lamp. A tingling sound whispered through the air as the tattered wings moved, then stilled, at peace. . . .

THE EDITOR'S CORNER

A critic once wrote that LOVESWEPT books have "the most off-the-wall titles" of any romance line. And recently, I got a letter from a reader asking me who is responsible for the "unusual titles" of our books. (Our fans are so polite; I'll bet she wanted to substitute "strange" for unusual!) Whether off-the-wall or unusual—I prefer to think of them as memorable—our titles are dreamed up by authors as well as editors. (We editors must take the responsibility for the most outrageous titles, though.) Next month you can look forward to six wonderful LOVESWEPTs that are as original, strong, amusing—yes, even as off-the-wall—as their titles.

First, **McKNIGHT IN SHINING ARMOR,** LOVESWEPT #276, by Tami Hoag, is an utterly heartwarming story of a young divorced woman, Kelsie Connors, who has two children to raise while holding down two *very* unusual jobs. She's trying to be the complete Superwoman when she meets hero Alec McKnight. Their first encounter, while hilarious, holds the potential for disaster . . . as black lace lingerie flies through the air of the conservative advertising executive's office. But Alec is enchanted, not enraged—and then Kelsie has to wonder if the "disaster" isn't what he's done to her heart. A joyous reading experience.

SHOWDOWN AT LIZARD ROCK, LOVESWEPT #277, by Sandra Chastain, features one of the most gorgeous and exciting pairs of lovers ever. Kaylyn Smith has the body of Wonder Woman and the face of Helen of Troy, and handsome hunk King Vandergriff realizes the

(continued)

moment he sets eyes on her that he's met his match. She is standing on top of Lizard Rock, protesting his construction company's building of a private club on the town's landmark. King just climbs right up there and carries her down . . . but she doesn't surrender. (Well, not immediately.) You'll delight in the feisty shenanigans of this marvelous couple.

CALIFORNIA ROYALE, LOVESWEPT #278, by Deborah Smith, is one of the most heart-stoppingly beautiful of love stories. Shea Somerton is elegant and glamorous just like the resort she runs; Duke Araiza is sexy and fast just like the Thoroughbreds he raises and trains. Both have heartbreaking pain in their pasts. And each has the fire and the understanding that the other needs. But their goals put them at cross-purposes, and neither of them can bend . . . until a shadow from Shea's early days falls over their lives. A thrilling romance.

Get out the box of tissues when you settle down to enjoy **WINTER'S DAUGHTER,** LOVESWEPT #279, by Kathleen Creighton, because you're bound to get a good laugh and a good cry from this marvelous love story. Tannis Winter, disguised as a bag-lady, has gone out onto the streets to learn about the plight of the homeless and to search for cures for their ills. But so has town councilman Dillon James, a "derelict" with mysterious attractions for the unknowing Tannis. Dillon is instantly bewitched by her courage and compassion . . . by the scent of summer on her skin and the brilliance of winter in her eyes. Their hunger for each other grows quickly . . . and to ravenous proportions. Only a risky confrontation can clear up the misunderstandings they face, so that they can finally have it all. We think you're going to treasure this very rich and very dramatic love story.

Completing the celebration of her fifth year as a published writer, the originator of continuing character romances, Iris Johansen, gives us the breathlessly emotional love story of the Sheik you met this month, exciting Damon El Karim, in **STRONG, HOT WINDS,** LOVESWEPT #280. Damon has vowed to punish the lovely Cory Brandel, the mother of his son, whom she's kept secret from him. To do so, he has her kidnapped with the

(continued)

boy and brought to Kasmara. But in his desert palace, as they set each other off, his sense of barbaric justice and her fury at his betrayal quickly turn into quite different emotions. Bewildered by the tenderness and the wild need he feels for her, Damon fears he can never have Cory's love. But at last, Cory has begun to understand what makes this complex and charismatic man tick—and she fears she isn't strong enough to give him the enduring love he so much deserves! Crème de la crème from Iris Johansen. I'm sure you join all of us at Bantam in wishing her not five, but *fifty* more years of creating great love stories!

Closing out the month in a very big way is **PARADISE CAFE,** LOVESWEPT #281, by Adrienne Staff. And what a magnificent tale this is. Beautiful Abby Clarke is rescued by ruggedly handsome outdoorsman Jack Gallagher—a man of few words and fast moves, especially when trying to haul in the lady whom destiny has put in his path. But Abby is not a risk taker. She's an earnest, hardworking young woman who's always put her family first . . . but Jack is an impossible man to walk away from with his sweet, wild passion that makes her yearn to forget about being safe. And Jack is definitely *not* safe for Abby . . . he's a man with wandering feet. You'll relish the way the stay-at-home and the vagabond find that each has a home in the center of the other's heart. A true delight.

I trust that you'll agree with me that the six LOVE-SWEPTs next month are as memorable as their off-the-wall titles!

Enjoy!

Carolyn Nichols

Carolyn Nichols
  Editor
LOVESWEPT
Bantam Books
666 Fifth Avenue
New York, NY 10103

THE HOMETOWN HUNK CONTEST

FOR EVERY WOMAN WHO HAS EVER SAID—
"I know a man who looks
just like the hero of this book"
—HAVE WE GOT A CONTEST FOR YOU!

To help celebrate our fifth year of publishing LOVESWEPT
we are having a fabulous, fun-filled event called THE
HOMETOWN HUNK contest. We are going to reissue six
classic early titles by six of your favorite authors.

DARLING OBSTACLES by Barbara Boswell
IN A CLASS BY ITSELF by Sandra Brown
C.J.'S FATE by Kay Hooper
THE LADY AND THE UNICORN by Iris Johansen
CHARADE by Joan Elliott Pickart
FOR THE LOVE OF SAMI by Fayrene Preston

Here, as in the backs of all July, August, and September
1988 LOVESWEPTS you will find "cover notes" just like the
ones we prepare at Bantam as the background for our art
director to create our covers. These notes will describe the
hero and heroine, give a teaser on the plot, and suggest a
scene for the cover. Your part in the contest will be to see
if a great looking local man—or men, if your hometown is
so blessed—fits our description of one of the heroes of the
six books we will reissue.

THE HOMETOWN HUNK who is selected (one for each of
the six titles) will be flown to New York via United Airlines
and will stay at the Loews Summit Hotel—the ideal hotel
for business or pleasure in midtown Manhattan—for two
nights. All travel arrangements made by Reliable Travel
International, Incorporated. He will be the model for the
new cover of the book which will be released in mid-1989.
The six people who send in the winning photos of their
HOMETOWN HUNK will receive a pre-selected assortment
of LOVESWEPT books free for one year. Please see the
Official Rules above the Official Entry Form for full details
and restrictions.

We can't wait to start judging those pictures! Oh, and you must let the man you've chosen know that you're entering him in the contest. After all, if he wins he'll have to come to New York.

Have fun. Here's your chance to get the cover-lover of your dreams!

Carolyn Nichols

Carolyn Nichols
Editor
LOVESWEPT
Bantam Books
666 Fifth Avenue
New York, NY 10102—0023

THE HOMETOWN HUNK CONTEST

DARLING OBSTACLES
(Originally Published as LOVESWEPT #95)
By Barbara Boswell

COVER NOTES

The Characters:

Hero:
GREG WILDER's gorgeous body and "to-die-for" good looks haven't hurt him in the dating department, but when most women discover he's a widower with four kids, they head for the hills! Greg has the hard, muscular build of an athlete, and his light brown hair, which he wears neatly parted on the side, is streaked blond by the sun. Add to that his aquamarine blue eyes that sparkle when he laughs, and his sensual mouth and generous lower lip, and you're probably wondering what woman in her right mind wouldn't want Greg's strong, capable surgeon's hands working their magic on her—kids or no kids!

Personality Traits:
An acclaimed neurosurgeon, Greg Wilder is a celebrity of sorts in the planned community of Woodland, Maryland. Authoritative, debonair, self-confident, his reputation for engaging in one casual relationship after another almost overshadows his prowess as a doctor. In reality, Greg dates more out of necessity than anything else, since he has to attend one social function after another. He considers most of the events boring and wishes he could spend more time with his children. But his profession is a difficult and demanding one—and being both father and mother to four kids isn't any less so. A thoughtful, generous, sometimes befuddled father, Greg tries to do it all. Cerebral, he uses his intellect and skill rather than physical strength to win his victories. However, he never expected to come up against one Mary Magdalene May!

Heroine:
MARY MAGDALENE MAY, called Maggie by her friends, is the thirty-two-year-old mother of three children. She has shoulder-length auburn hair, and green eyes that shout her Irish heritage. With high cheekbones and an upturned nose covered with a smattering of freckles, Maggie thinks of herself more as the girl-next-door type. Certainly, she believes, she could never be one of Greg Wilder's beautiful escorts.

Setting: The small town of Woodland, Maryland

The Story:
Surgeon Greg Wilder wanted to court the feisty and beautiful widow who'd been caring for his four kids, but she just wouldn't let him past her doorstep! Sure that his interest was only casual, and that he preferred more sophisticated women, Maggie May vowed to keep Greg at arm's length. But he wouldn't take no for an answer. And once he'd crashed through her defenses and pulled her into his arms, he was tireless—and reckless—in his campaign to win her over. Maggie had found it tough enough to resist one determined doctor; now he threatened to call in his kids and hers as reinforcements—seven rowdy snags to romance!

Cover scene:
As if romancing Maggie weren't hard enough, Greg can't seem to find time to spend with her without their children around. Stealing a private moment on the stairs in Maggie's house, Greg and Maggie embrace. She is standing one step above him, but she still has to look up at him to see into his eyes. Greg's hands are on her hips, and her hands are resting on his shoulders. Maggie is wearing a very sheer, short pink nightgown, and Greg has on wheat-colored jeans and a navy and yellow striped rugby shirt. Do they have time to kiss?

THE HOMETOWN HUNK CONTEST

IN A CLASS BY ITSELF
(Originally Published as LOVESWEPT #66)
By Sandra Brown

COVER NOTES

The Characters:

Hero:
LOGAN WEBSTER would have no trouble posing for a
Scandinavian travel poster. His wheat-colored hair always
seems to be tousled, defying attempts to control it, and
falls across his wide forehead. Thick eyebrows one shade
darker than his hair accentuate his crystal blue eyes. He
has a slender nose that flairs slightly over a mouth that
testifies to both sensitivity and strength. The faint lines
around his eyes and alongside his mouth give the impression that reaching the ripe age of 30 wasn't all fun and
games for him. Logan's square, determined jaw is punctu-
ated by a vertical cleft. His broad shoulders and narrow
waist add to his tall, lean appearance.

Personality traits:
Logan Webster has had to scrape and save and fight for
everything he's gotten. Born into a poor farm family, he
was driven to succeed and overcome his "wrong side of
the tracks" image. His businesses include cattle, real estate, and natural gas. Now a pillar of the community,
Logan's life has been a true rags-to-riches story. Only
Sandra Brown's own words can describe why he is masculinity epitomized: "Logan had 'the walk,' that saddle-
tramp saunter that was inherent to native Texan men,
passed down through generations of cowboys. It was, without even trying to be, sexy. The unconscious roll of the
hips, the slow strut, the flexed knees, the slouching stance,
the deceptive laziness that hid a latent aggressiveness."
Wow! And not only does he have "the walk," but he's fun

and generous and kind. Even with his wealth, he feels at home living in his small hometown with simple, hard-working, middle-class, backbone-of-America folks. A born leader, people automatically gravitate toward him.

Heroine:
DANI QUINN is a sophisticated twenty-eight-year-old woman. Dainty, her body compact, she is utterly feminine. Dani's pale, lustrous hair is moonlight and honey spun together, and because it is very straight, she usually wears it in a chignon. With golden eyes to match her golden hair, Dani is the one woman Logan hasn't been able to get off his mind for the ten years they've been apart.

Setting: Primarily on Logan's ranch in East Texas.

The Story:
Ten years had passed since Dani Quinn had graduated from high school in the small Texas town, ten years since the night her elopement with Logan Webster had ended in disaster. Now Dani approached her tenth reunion with uncertainty. Logan would be there . . . Logan, the only man who'd ever made her shiver with desire and need, but would she have the courage to face the fury in his eyes? She couldn't defend herself against his anger and hurt—to do so would demand she reveal the secret sorrow she shared with no one. Logan's touch had made her his so long ago. Could he reach past the pain to make her his for all time?

Cover Scene:
It's sunset, and Logan and Dani are standing beside the swimming pool on his ranch, embracing. The pool is surrounded by semitropical plants and lush flower beds. In the distance, acres of rolling pasture land resembling a green lake undulate into dense, piney woods. Dani is wearing a strapless, peacock blue bikini and sandals with leather ties that wrap around her ankles. Her hair is straight and loose, falling to the middle of her back. Logan has on a light-colored pair of corduroy shorts and a short-sleeved designer knit shirt in a pale shade of yellow.

THE HOMETOWN HUNK CONTEST

C.J.'S FATE
(Originally Published as LOVESWEPT #32)
By Kay Hooper

COVER NOTES

The Characters:

Hero:
FATE WESTON easily could have walked straight off an
Indian reservation. His raven black hair and strong, well-
molded features testify to his heritage. But somewhere
along the line genetics threw Fate a curve—his eyes are
the deepest, darkest blue imaginable! Above those blue
eyes are dark slanted eyebrows, and fanning out from
those eyes are faint laugh lines—the only sign of the fact
that he's thirty-four years old. Tall, Fate moves with easy,
loose-limbed grace. Although he isn't an athlete, Fate takes
very good care of himself, and it shows in his strong
physique. Striking at first glance and fascinating with
each succeeding glance, the serious expressions on his
face make him look older than his years, but with one
smile he looks boyish again.

Personality traits:
Fate possesses a keen sense of humor. His heavy-lidded,
intelligent eyes are capable of concealment, but there is a
shrewdness in them that reveals the man hadn't needed
college or a law degree to be considered intelligent. The set
of his head tells you that he is proud—perhaps even a bit
arrogant. He is attractive and perfectly well aware of that
fact. Unconventional, paradoxical, tender, silly, lusty, gentle, comical, serious, absurd, and endearing are all words
that come to mind when you think of Fate. He is not
ashamed to be everything a man can be. A defense attorney by profession, one can detect a bit of frustrated actor
in his character. More than anything else, though, it's the

impression of humor about him—reinforced by the elusive dimple in his cheek—that makes Fate Weston a scrumptious hero!

Heroine:
C.J. ADAMS is a twenty-six-year-old research librarian. Unaware of her own attractiveness, C.J. tends to play down her pixylike figure and tawny gold eyes. But once she meets Fate, she no longer feels that her short, burnished copper curls and the sprinkling of freckles on her nose make her unappealing. He brings out the vixen in her, and changes the smart, bookish woman who professed to have no interest in men into the beautiful, sexy woman she really was all along. Now, if only he could get her to tell him what C.J. stands for!

Setting: Ski lodge in Aspen, Colorado

The Story:
C.J. Adams had been teased enough about her seeming lack of interest in the opposite sex. On a ski trip with her five best friends, she impulsively embraced a handsome stranger, pretending they were secret lovers—and the delighted lawyer who joined in her impetuous charade seized the moment to deepen the kiss. Astonished at his reaction, C.J. tried to nip their romance in the bud—but found herself nipping at his neck instead! She had met her match in a man who could answer her witty remarks with clever ripostes of his own, and a lover whose caresses aroused in her a passionate need she'd never suspected that she could feel. Had destiny somehow tossed them together?

Cover Scene:
C.J. and Fate virtually have the ski slopes to themselves early one morning, and they take advantage of it! Frolicking in a snow drift, Fate is covering C.J. with snow—and kisses! They are flushed from the cold weather and from the excitement of being in love. C.J. is wearing a sky-blue, one-piece, tight-fitting ski outfit that zips down the front. Fate is wearing a navy blue parka and matching ski pants.

THE HOMETOWN HUNK CONTEST

THE LADY AND THE UNICORN
(Originally Published as LOVESWEPT #29)
By Iris Johansen

COVER NOTES

The Characters:

Hero:
Not classically handsome, RAFE SANTINE's blunt, craggy features reinforce the quality of overpowering virility about him. He has wide, Slavic cheekbones and a bold, thrusting chin, which give the impression of strength and authority. Thick black eyebrows are set over piercing dark eyes. He wears his heavy, dark hair long. His large frame measures in at almost six feet four inches, and it's hard to believe that a man with such brawny shoulders and strong thighs could exhibit the pantherlike grace which characterizes Rafe's movements. Rafe Santine is definitely a man to be reckoned with, and heroine Janna Cannon does just that!

Personality traits:
Our hero is a man who radiates an aura of power and danger, and women find him intriguing and irresistible. Rafe Santine is a self-made billionaire at the age of thirty-eight. Almost entirely self-educated, he left school at sixteen to work on his first construction job, and by the time he was twenty-three, he owned the company. From there he branched out into real estate, computers, and oil. Rafe reportedly changes mistresses as often as he changes shirts. His reputation for ruthless brilliance has been earned over years of fighting to the top of the economic ladder from the slums of New York. His gruff manner and hard personality hide the tender, vulnerable side of him. Rafe also possesses an insatiable thirst for knowledge that is a passion with him. Oddly enough, he has a wry sense of

humor that surfaces unexpectedly from time to time. And, though cynical to the extreme, he never lets his natural skepticism interfere with his innate sense of justice.

Heroine:
JANNA CANNON, a game warden for a small wildlife preserve, is a very dedicated lady. She is tall at five feet nine inches and carries herself in a stately way. Her long hair is dark brown and is usually twisted into a single thick braid in back. Of course, Rafe never lets her keep her hair braided when they make love! Janna is one quarter Cherokee Indian by heritage, and she possesses the dark eyes and skin of her ancestors.

Setting: Rafe's estate in Carmel, California

The Story:
Janna Cannon scaled the high walls of Rafe Santine's private estate, afraid of nothing and determined to appeal to the powerful man who could save her beloved animal preserve. She bewitched his guard dogs, then cast a spell of enchantment over him as well. Janna's profound grace, her caring nature, made the tough and proud Rafe grow mercurial in her presence. She offered him a gift he'd never risked reaching out for before—but could he trust his own emotions enough to open himself to her love?

Cover Scene:
In the gazebo overlooking the rugged cliffs at the edge of the Pacific Ocean, Rafe and Janna share a passionate moment together. The gazebo is made of redwood and the interior is small and cozy. Scarlet cushions cover the benches, and matching scarlet curtains hang from the eaves, caught back by tasseled sashes to permit the sea breeze to whip through the enclosure. Rafe is wearing black suede pants and a charcoal gray crew-neck sweater. Janna is wearing a safari-style khaki shirt-and-slacks outfit and suede desert boots. They embrace against the breathtaking backdrop of wild, crashing, white-crested waves pounding the rocks and cliffs below.

THE HOMETOWN HUNK CONTEST

CHARADE
(Originally Published as LOVESWEPT #74)
By Joan Elliott Pickart

COVER NOTES

The Characters:

Hero:
The phrase tall, dark, and handsome was coined to describe TENNES WHITNEY. His coal black hair reaches past his collar in back, and his fathomless steel gray eyes are framed by the kind of thick, dark lashes that a woman would kill to have. Darkly tanned, Tennes has a straight nose and a square chin, with—you guessed it!—a Kirk Douglas cleft. Tennes oozes masculinity and virility. He's a handsome son-of-a-gun!

Personality traits:
A shrewd, ruthless business tycoon, Tennes is a man of strength and principle. He's perfected the art of buying floundering companies and turning them around financially, then selling them at a profit. He possesses a sixth sense about business—in short, he's a winner! But there are two sides to his personality. Always in cool command, Tennes, who fears no man or challenge, is rendered emotionally vulnerable when faced with his elderly aunt's illness. His deep devotion to the woman who raised him clearly casts him as a warm, compassionate guy—not at all like the tough-as-nails executive image he presents. Leave it to heroine Whitney Jordan to discover the real man behind the complicated enigma.

Heroine:
WHITNEY JORDAN's russet-colored hair floats past her shoulders in glorious waves. Her emerald green eyes, full breasts, and long, slender legs—not to mention her peaches-

and-cream complexion—make her eye-poppingly attractive. How can Tennes resist the twenty-six-year-old beauty? And how can Whitney consider becoming serious with him? If their romance flourishes, she may end up being Whitney Whitney!

Setting: Los Angeles, California

The Story:
One moment writer Whitney Jordan was strolling the aisles of McNeil's Department Store, plotting the untimely demise of a soap opera heartthrob; the next, she was nearly knocked over by a real-life stunner who implored her to be his fiancée! The ailing little gray-haired aunt who'd raised him had one final wish, he said—to see her dear nephew Tennes married to the wonderful girl he'd described in his letters . . . only that girl hadn't existed—until now! Tennes promised the masquerade would last only through lunch, but Whitney gave such an inspired performance that Aunt Olive refused to let her go. And what began as a playful romantic deception grew more breathlessly real by the minute. . . .

Cover Scene:
Whitney's living room is bright and cheerful. The gray carpeting and blue sofa with green and blue throw pillows gives the apartment a cool but welcoming appearance. Sitting on the sofa next to Tennes, Whitney is wearing a black crepe dress that is simply cut but stunning. It is cut low over her breasts and held at the shoulders by thin straps. The skirt falls to her knees in soft folds and the bodice is nipped in at the waist with a matching belt. She has on black high heels, but prefers not to wear any jewelry to spoil the simplicity of the dress. Tennes is dressed in a black suit with a white silk shirt and a deep red tie.

THE HOMETOWN HUNK CONTEST

FOR THE LOVE OF SAMI
(Originally Published as LOVESWEPT #34)
By Fayrene Preston

COVER NOTES

Hero:
DANIEL PARKER-ST. JAMES is every woman's dream come true. With glossy black hair and warm, reassuring blue eyes, he makes our heroine melt with just a glance. Daniel's lean face is chiseled into assertive planes. His lips are full and firmly sculptured, and his chin has the determined and arrogant thrust to it only a man who's sure of himself can carry off. Daniel has a lot in common with Clark Kent. Both wear glasses, and when Daniel removes them to make love to Sami, she thinks he really is Superman!

Personality traits:
Daniel Parker-St. James is one of the Twin Cities' most respected attorneys. He's always in the news, either in the society columns with his latest society lady, or on the front page with his headline cases. He's brilliant and takes on only the toughest cases—usually those that involve millions of dollars. Daniel has a reputation for being a deadly opponent in the courtroom. Because he's from a socially prominent family and is a Harvard graduate, it's expected that he'll run for the Senate one day. Distinguished-looking and always distinctively dressed—he's fastidious about his appearance—Daniel gives off an unassailable air of authority and absolute control.

Heroine:
SAMUELINA (SAMI) ADKINSON is secretly a wealthy heiress. No one would guess. She lives in a converted warehouse loft, dresses to suit no one but herself, and dabbles in the creative arts. Sami is twenty-six years old, with

long, honey-colored hair. She wears soft, wispy bangs and has very thick brown lashes framing her golden eyes. Of medium height, Sami has to look up to gaze into Daniel's deep blue eyes.

Setting: St. Paul, Minnesota

The Story:
Unpredictable heiress Sami Adkinson had endeared herself to the most surprising people—from the bag ladies in the park she protected . . . to the mobster who appointed himself her guardian . . . to her exasperated but loving friends. Then Sami was arrested while demonstrating to save baby seals, and it took powerful attorney Daniel Parker-St. James to bail her out. Daniel was smitten, soon cherishing Sami and protecting her from her night fears. Sami reveled in his love—and resisted it too. And holding on to Sami, Daniel discovered, was like trying to hug quicksilver. . . .

Cover Scene:
The interior of Daniel's house is very grand and supremely formal, the decor sophisticated, refined, and quietly tasteful, just like Daniel himself. Rich traditional fabrics cover plush oversized custom sofas and Regency wing chairs. Queen Anne furniture is mixed with Chippendale and is subtly complemented with Oriental accent pieces. In the library, floor-to-ceiling bookcases filled with rare books provide the backdrop for Sami and Daniel's embrace. Sami is wearing a gold satin sheath gown. The dress has a high neckline, but in back is cut provocatively to the waist. Her jewels are exquisite. The necklace is made up of clusters of flowers created by large, flawless diamonds. From every cluster a huge, perfectly matched teardrop emerald hangs. The earrings are composed of an even larger flower cluster, and an equally huge teardrop-shaped emerald hangs from each one. Daniel is wearing a classic, elegant tuxedo.

LOVESWEPT® HOMETOWN HUNK CONTEST

OFFICIAL RULES

IN A CLASS BY ITSELF by Sandra Brown
FOR THE LOVE OF SAMI by Fayrene Preston
C.J.'S FATE by Kay Hooper
THE LADY AND THE UNICORN by Iris Johansen
CHARADE by Joan Elliott Pickart
DARLING OBSTACLES by Barbara Boswell

1. NO PURCHASE NECESSARY. Enter the HOMETOWN HUNK contest by completing the Official Entry Form below and enclosing a sharp color full-length photograph (easy to see details, with the photo being no smaller than 2½″ × 3½″) of the man you think perfectly represents one of the heroes from the above-listed books which are described in the accompanying Loveswept cover notes. Please be sure to fill out the Official Entry Form completely, and also be sure to clearly print on the back of the man's photograph the man's name, address, city, state, zip code, telephone number, date of birth, your name, address, city, state, zip code, telephone number, your relationship, if any, to the man (e.g. wife, girlfriend) as well as the title of the Loveswept book for which you are entering the man. If you do not have an Official Entry Form, you can print all of the required information on a 3″ × 5″ card and attach it to the photograph with all the necessary information printed on the back of the photograph as well. YOUR HERO MUST SIGN BOTH THE BACK OF THE OFFICIAL ENTRY FORM (OR 3″ × 5″ CARD) AND THE PHOTOGRAPH TO SIGNIFY HIS CONSENT TO BEING ENTERED IN THE CONTEST. Completed entries should be sent to:

BANTAM BOOKS
HOMETOWN HUNK CONTEST
Department CN
666 Fifth Avenue
New York, New York 10102–0023

All photographs and entries become the property of Bantam Books and will not be returned under any circumstances.

2. Six men will be chosen by the Loveswept authors as a HOMETOWN HUNK (one HUNK per Loveswept title). By entering the contest, each winner and each person who enters a winner agrees to abide by Bantam Books' rules and to be subject to Bantam Books' eligibility requirements. Each winning HUNK and each person who enters a winner will be required to sign all papers deemed necessary by Bantam Books before receiving any prize. Each winning HUNK will be flown via **United Airlines** from his closest United Airlines-serviced city to New York City and will stay at the ꟽ SꞨNꞮꞮ Hotel—the ideal hotel for business or pleasure in midtown Manhattan—for two nights. Winning HUNKS' meals and hotel transfers will be provided by Bantam Books. Travel and hotel arrangements are made by *RELIABLE TRAVEL INTERNATIONAL* and are subject to availability and to Bantam Books' date requirements. Each winning HUNK will pose with a female model at a photographer's studio for a photograph that will serve as the basis of a Loveswept front cover. Each winning HUNK will receive a $150.00 modeling fee. Each winning HUNK will be required to sign an Affidavit of Eligibility and Model's Release supplied by Bantam Books. (Approximate retail value of HOMETOWN HUNK'S PRIZE: $900.00). The six people who send in a winning HOMETOWN HUNK photograph that is used by Bantam will receive free for one year each, LOVESWEPT romance paperback books published by Bantam during that year. (Approximate retail value: $180.00.) Each person who submits a winning photograph

will also be required to sign an Affidavit of Eligibility and Promotional Release supplied by Bantam Books. All winning HUNKS' (as well as the people who submit the winning photographs) names, addresses, biographical data and likenesses may be used by Bantam Books for publicity and promotional purposes without any additional compensation. There will be no prize substitutions or cash equivalents made.

3. All completed entries must be received by Bantam Books no later than September 15, 1988. Bantam Books is not responsible for lost or misdirected entries. The finalists will be selected by Loveswept editors and the six winning HOMETOWN HUNKS will be selected by the six authors of the participating Loveswept books. Winners will be selected on the basis of how closely the judges believe they reflect the descriptions of the books' heroes. Winners will be notified on or about October 31, 1988. If there are insufficient entries or if in the judges' opinions, no entry is suitable or adequately reflects the descriptions of the hero(s) in the book(s), Bantam may decide not to award a prize for the applicable book(s) and may reissue the book(s) at its discretion.

4. The contest is open to residents of the U.S. and Canada, except the Province of Quebec, and is void where prohibited by law. All federal and local regulations apply. Employees of Reliable Travel International, Inc., United Airlines, the Summit Hotel, and the Bantam Doubleday Dell Publishing Group, Inc., their subsidiaries and affiliates, and their immediate families are ineligible to enter.

5. For an extra copy of the Official Rules, the Official Entry Form, and the accompanying Loveswept cover notes, send your request and a self-addressed stamped envelope (Vermont and Washington State residents need not affix postage) before August 20, 1988 to the address listed in Paragraph 1 above.

LOVESWEPT® HOMETOWN HUNK OFFICIAL ENTRY FORM

BANTAM BOOKS
HOMETOWN HUNK CONTEST
Dept. CN
666 Fifth Avenue
New York, New York 10102–0023

HOMETOWN HUNK CONTEST

YOUR NAME_____

YOUR ADDRESS_____

CITY_____ STATE_____ ZIP_____

THE NAME OF THE LOVESWEPT BOOK FOR WHICH YOU ARE ENTERING THIS PHOTO

_____by_____

YOUR RELATIONSHIP TO YOUR HERO_____

YOUR HERO'S NAME_____

YOUR HERO'S ADDRESS_____

CITY_____ STATE_____ ZIP_____

YOUR HERO'S TELEPHONE #_____

YOUR HERO'S DATE OF BIRTH_____

YOUR HERO'S SIGNATURE CONSENTING TO HIS PHOTOGRAPH ENTRY

_____

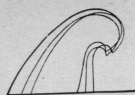

LOVESWEPT

Love Stories you'll never forget by authors you'll always remember

☐	21877	**Stiff Competition #234** Doris Parmett	$2.50
☐	21867	**Too Hot To Handle #235** Sandra Chastain	$2.50
☐	21868	**Sharing Secrets #236** Barbara Boswell	$2.50
☐	21870	**Unmasking Kelsey #237** Kay Hooper	$2.50
☐	21869	**Midsummer Sorcery #238** Joan Elliott Pickart	$2.50
☐	21878	**The Prince and the Patriot #239** Kathleen Creighton	$2.50
☐	21866	**Cajun Nights #240** Susan Richardson	$2.50
☐	21871	**Travelin' Man #241** Charlotte Hughes	$2.50
☐	21883	**Intimate Details #242** Barbara Boswell	$2.50
☐	21884	**Kiss Me Again, Sam #243** Joan Elliott Pickart	$2.50
☐	21885	**Sapphire Lightning #244** Fayrene Preston	$2.50
☐	21886	**Jed's Sweet Revenge #245** Deborah Smith	$2.50
☐	21863	**The Widow and hte Wildcatter #246** Fran Baker	$2.50
☐	21887	**Silk On the Skin #247** Linda Cajio	$2.50
☐	21888	**The Object of His Affection #248** Sara Orwig	$2.50
☐	21889	**January in July #249** Joan Elliott Pickart	$2.50
☐	21882	**Let's Do It Again #250** Janet Bieber	$2.50
☐	21890	**The Luck of the Irish #251** Patt Bucheister	$2.50

Special Offer
Buy a Bantam Book
for only 50¢.

Now you can have Bantam's catalog filled with hundreds of titles plus take advantage of our unique and exciting bonus book offer. A special offer which gives you the opportunity to purchase a Bantam book for only 50¢. Here's how!

By ordering any five books at the regular price per order, you can also choose any other single book listed (up to a $5.95 value) for just 50¢. Some restrictions do apply, but for further details why not send for Bantam's catalog of titles today!

Just send us your name and address and we will send you a catalog!